# Shakespeare's Ripper

by Naomi Wallace Asher

H&P

# Shakespeare's Ripper

Fifth Revision, 2018



by NAOMI CLAIRE WALLACE

ISBN: 978-1-9997159-3-9

A catalogue record for this book is available from The British Library

Published by Hope & Plum Publishing
*www.hopeandplum.com*

**Prologue**

The girl ran through the rain, but it was no use. She was still choking from the stranglehold, and her throat had been badly cut. The footsteps behind her seemed to increase in volume, although the sound echoing in her ears could have been her heart pounding. Suddenly, a second man sprang out of the shadows and grabbed her arms. She tried to fight back, but the man tightened his grasp.

"You should stop squirming," he said calmly. "It will hurt more this way."

The voice echoed in her mind as she tried in struggled to free herself. She tried to scream but she found herself only sputtering blood. The echoing footsteps finally caught up to them, and the large hands once again enveloped her throat.

"Why are you doing this?" she choked.

"You are the first," came the response.

She heard the voice only dimly as the world went black.

The two men moved the girl back to the correct spot and laid her gently on the ground. Taking out a knife, they finished slicing her throat and set about carving her abdomen. Once they had finished their dissection, they removed the book from a rucksack, opened it to the marked page, and set it underneath the body.

"Well done, Brother."

The other man nodded, and they walked back through the rain to the black car that waited patiently in the shadows for them.

"We have four left."

## Chapter 1

**"There are more things in Heaven and earth, Horatio Than are dreamt of in your philosophy." - *Hamlet***

Charlie sat up suddenly and looked around. It took him a full minute before he remembered where he was. Only yesterday he had been at home in Maryland. Now he was in this strange room in a strange country. He fumbled for his watch, which he had reset on the plane. 4:45 AM. *Ugh*, he thought. *It'll take me forever to get used to the time difference, and when I finally do, it'll be time to go home.*

He swept his curly dark hair out of his sleepy blue eyes. He was still wearing the clothes he had worn on the plane. This had been his mother's idea; he hadn't wanted to come.

Every year, his college's theatre department gave an award to their best student: the Stafford Award. Charlie somehow managed to win it this year without even noticing. He had been so busy working on shows that he hadn't even realized how impressed the faculty had been with him. The Stafford Award gave one theatre student a scholarship to England to do something connected with the business of theatre. Each previous recipient had rushed to apply for the numerous summer programs, but Charlie just hadn't felt motivated enough to look into any specific program. Theatre was a passion to be sure, but he had been too busy to focus on any particular subject area. Finally, his mother suggested he go for a more general summer course. She had researched it for him and liked this one. The scholarship only stipulated theatre, but tradition encouraged a concrete learning experience. Following a number of weeks of gentle negotiating, it was agreed that he could do anything as long as his summer project culminated in his writing and producing a play. Producing was fine. He had been a production manager for three years at school.

"But write a play," he mumbled. How was he going to do that? He was a techie; how was he going to write anything that resembled a play?

He pulled himself out of bed, stepping on the *Engineering News* magazine he had been reading on the plane, and tried to turn on his light. It wouldn't turn on. He groaned.

"Some techie. I can't even turn on a light."

He looked at the plug and realized there was a switch that turned the socket on and off. He switched it on and then tried his lamp. It worked. He dragged himself to the sink in the corner of his dorm room and splashed water on his face. Looking in the mirror, he tried to rub some of the sleep marks away from his freckled cheeks. Finally, he shook off his grubby plane clothes and rummaged naked through his suitcase.

Once dressed, he wandered out of his room in search of food. He didn't know what would be open this early, but his stomach led him down the stairs and out into the cold misty air towards what he had thought was a convenience store. Closed. Out of luck, he walked further away from his building and the darkened shop, down the windy streets until he arrived at the riverbank. He stopped walking for a minute to gaze over the river towards the City of London.

*It really is beautiful*, he thought. The Thames at dawn sparkled in the glow of the riverboats and the reflection of the city lights, which managed to peek through the haze that hugged the city. Although it was June, the air was cold and damp. A quiet calm enveloped Charlie. He remained still for another minute, allowing himself to take in every detail. The dull lapping of the water against the riverbank kept rhythm with the hum of the late-night drivers and early morning commuters. Eventually he noticed a strange clicking sound emanating from somewhere nearby. He scanned and espied a blonde woman sitting on a bench, typing on a laptop. She appeared statuesque in the dim glow of the lights. Other than the rapping of her fingertips against the keyboard, she didn't move. He watched her curiously for a few moments. She paused in her typing to stare out at the water. Fascinated, he began walking towards her. Her head whipped around to glare at him, and he suddenly realized that 5:00 in the morning on a riverbank in a strange country was no time to really begin making friends. Frantically, he tried to think of something to say.

"Ummm," he stammered, "excuse me, I'm sorry, I really don't mean to bother you, but I, uh, I'm new here, in London I mean, and I was hungry and couldn't sleep, and well, do you know of any place to get any food around here?"

She stared back for a minute before answering, neither smiling nor glowering. "Nothing opens for at least another hour or so."

"You're American! The first person I've talked to here, and you're not even British."

She kept staring at him as if she was measuring him for something. "Did you come from the London School of Economics dorm over there? The LSE dorm, called Bankside?"

Charlie nodded awkwardly.

"Well, I think there's a vending machine in the basement; that's your best bet."

"You live in my building? I mean, I think..." He paused, stumbling over his words. She shifted her gaze back towards the water.

Charlie understood this to mean the conversation was over. Reluctantly he said, "Okay, thanks, I'm sorry to bother you."

With that he began the walk back to his dorm. The early morning summer sky was just beginning to lighten. Charlie stopped for a moment and turned back towards the girl. A strange scuffling noise forced his gaze towards one of the nearby buildings. For a moment he thought he saw a human shadow mixed in with the building's silhouette. He stared harder but saw nothing.

"I've been on a plane; I haven't slept. I'm definitely seeing things," he said out loud to himself. Looking over towards the bench, he realized the girl had gone. Oh well, he thought, and went back to his dorm to find the vending machine, and hopefully to return to sleep.

Behind him, the shadow detached itself from the wall of the building, cursing first the fact that the boy with the curly hair seemed to stare right at him, then at the fact that in his haste, he had smashed his toe against the bricks. Wincing in pain, he looked towards where she had been.

"Bugger, she's bloody quick," he complained to no one, and limped off to find her. What would the boss say if he found out he'd lost her again? *Can't let her out of my sight*, he thought, *not until it's time*.

## Chapter 2

**"Come what come may, time and the hour runs through the roughest day." - *Macbeth***

Charlie's alarm clock blared a few hours later. He slammed it silent and turned over, again momentarily forgetting where he was. Voices in the hallway brought his memory back into focus. Groggily, he rubbed the sleep out of his eyes. The first day of class—ugh. His thoughts floated back to the bridge, or the boardwalk—whatever that area along the river was called. The blonde girl, no, woman... His cheeks reddened just thinking about it. He had really made a fool of himself. No wonder she had been so reluctant to talk to him. What kind of idiot goes up to a stranger in the middle of the night and babbles about food and nationalities? He wondered if she lived in his building. There were loads of apartments around, but she had been right about the vending machine. He tried to shrug it off.

He didn't go to LSE. His program was run through a university in the States. They used this dorm to house their students. Yesterday he had seen a ton of other college-age students and had wondered whether they were all part of his course. For that matter, was the woman on the bench part of his course? Well, he'd find out soon enough. His class was supposed to have their first meeting in less than an hour. Charlie raised himself out of bed and showered in what was perhaps the smallest shower he had ever seen. Finally feeling clean, he dressed for the second time in four hours.

Downstairs Charlie found the cafeteria. Thankfully, breakfast was included in the program. No other meals were, however, and he made a mental note to find a store and buy some food to keep in his room just in case. The strong aroma of eggs and bacon led him into a dining room filled with one hundred or so students and a few older people who looked like teachers. He piled his plate with fried eggs, fried bread, oddly fatless bacon and hash brown potatoes, grabbed a cup of coffee and sat down among them. Nearly all of them were American, and one girl was speaking loudly about how excited she was to be there. She was obviously from the south. Even if her accent didn't give her away, her t-shirt read, "Save Up Your Confederate Money, Boys, The South Will Rise Again."

"I can't believe it!" she shouted. "Can you imagine? Little old me! Here! Aren't y'all excited?"

She turned to Charlie and continued to shout. "I'm Mary Jo White from Pensacola, Florida. I'm here for the King's College program! What's your name?"

"Charlie," he grumbled. "Same course."

"Ooohhh!" she shrieked. "We are gonna be classmates! I can tell we'll be best friends! Y'know, you are just the cutest thing!"

With that she gave him a big hug and turned to the people at the next table. Pointing to Charlie, she bellowed to them, "This one's here, too! I can't wait. This is gonna be the best time ever! I'm more excited than a cow at milking time!"

The others didn't seem to find her as annoying as he did, so he just sat quietly eating while Mary Jo entertained the room with excruciatingly loud stories about how she had dreamed of this her whole life, and continually questioning whether everyone was everyone.

He was so preoccupied with his breakfast and trying to ignore Mary Jo that he didn't notice the blonde woman from the bench approach and sit across from him.

"She is the reason the British don't like Americans," the blonde muttered to Charlie. The sound of her voice startled him. He looked up questioningly.

"Hi there, um, you live here, too? I, well, I…" The words lodged themselves in Charlie's throat while his eyes focused on the intriguing woman across from him. She was clearly not a student and seemed out of place somehow.

"I'm Arden," she said. "I'm sorry about this morning. I was trying to work on something and needed a break, so I went to sit by the river. My mind was drifting, and I didn't know who you were. I hope you found the vending machine."

"It's okay, I didn't mean to surprise you. I don't usually talk to strangers in the middle of the night, I swear. My name's Charlie. Are you here for the King's College course?"

Before she could respond, an older man whom Charlie recognized as the program advisor, Mr. Hendry, appeared and announced that all King's College students were to report directly to the common room in the basement. Charlie turned back to the woman, but she had somehow disappeared. Again. He looked frantically across the room and finally located her standing next to Mr. Hendry. He took one last stab at his breakfast, drank some coffee, and rose to join his group.

## Chapter 3

**"Our doubts are traitors, And make us lose the good we oft might win, By fearing to attempt." -** ***Measure for Measure***

The darkness was chasing them. Closing in. Faster and faster. "Grab my hand!" he yelled. His brother clung to him, panting, his small legs moving as fast as they could. Where was she? "Mum? Mum, where are you?" he yelled. "We're here! We're coming!" The corridor wove around like a maze, each turn promising an end that never came. Their fear sped up and so did the boys' steps. Faster, faster, he ran, dragging his little brother. Faster around the turns, up and down the stairs, out to the street, around the buildings, faster, and faster, screaming for her. He could help her, he could save her. Then finally, the door. He held out his hand to open it, and...

Peter woke up screaming. He looked around frantically before remembering that it was the dream. The same dream, in fact, that plagued him nightly. Sometimes it wasn't as bad. When he was happy... in a relationship... it even went away for a w3hile; but it always came back. That same night so many years ago. The night his mother was killed.

He looked at his watch.

"Bollocks!" he exclaimed, cursing his own tiredness. He was supposed to be there half an hour ago. His toe still hurt from the night, or early morning, before. After losing the girl, he had decided to get some much-needed rest. He knew she had a meeting in the morning and he figured he'd find her there. A good thought, except now he was late. The phone rang.

"'Ello, Gov. I was just on me way out," Peter said lightly.

"You should be there already. We need to keep an eye on her. You know what happened last night."

Peter's mind drifted to the image of the dead girl.

"Y'sir, Gov, and I'm on me way.'

"Good. And you're sure she doesn't know you're following her?"

"She's got no idea, Gov."

"Keep it that way," came the voice. The line went dead.

## Chapter 4

**"The more pity that fools may not speak wisely what wise men do foolishly." – *As You Like It***

Once the group was assembled, Charlie took a good look at his mysterious blonde who was now sitting alone in the corner of the room. She didn't look much older than him, but she had something about her that made her look more... mature? She was wearing jeans, boots, and a colorful patchwork corduroy blazer with a thin scarf and a black t-shirt that read "RIPPER" in white letters. Her bleached blond hair fell in two long braids that gave her an artsy look. Mary Jo would have looked really stupid in an outfit like that, but this woman looked intelligent. And beautiful. Wow, he thought, who would think that Pippi Longstocking braids could manage to make a girl look smart?

"Excuse me; settle down, students," Mr. Hendry commanded. He didn't need to say much more before the whole room was quiet and waiting. There were not as many students involved in the program as Charlie had originally thought. Only about twenty of the people eating breakfast had assembled in the common room.

"I am Richard Hendry. I will be your course leader. As you can see, there are many different programmes that utilize this domestic accommodation. It is my expectation that you will all respect the generosity that the LSE has demonstrated in allowing us to temporarily inhabit its facility. Today we will be giving course assignments and taking a tour of the area. After today, you are to report directly to your course advisor in the location assigned. There are various group events scheduled, which will involve all of you, but in general you will spend your time in your smaller groups. This room is the LSE dorm pub. It opens at 5 PM and closes at 11:30 PM daily. I will be here every evening at 6:30 PM if you have any questions. In order to assign specific courses, you were asked prior to arriving to fill out a short questionnaire. Based on your answers, you will now be given your class assignments."

"Mr. Handly? Oh, Mr. Handly!" Mary Jo was practically jumping out of her seat.

"It's Mr. Hendry, and yes, Miss..."

"White, Mary Jo White from Pensacola, Florida."

"Yes, Miss White, what can I do for you?"

Completely oblivious to his disdain, Mary Jo continued.

"Did we all get our first choices? I'll just die if I didn't. Some of the choices looked so historic."

A few snickers echoed through the room, but when Mr. Hendry informed them that not all first choices were available, most of the sound changed to anxious whispers.

"As you can see," Mr. Hendry continued, "there are a few visiting professors present who are here to whisk you off to your respective locations."

None of them had noticed before, but now, as Charlie looked around, he saw they had been joined by five strangers. Charlie looked at his course list and counted six courses. He didn't see Mr. Hendry's name listed as teaching a course. Mary Jo also noticed the inconsistency.

"Mr. H.? Are you teaching one of the classes? I see there are five teachers, but six classes."

"It's Hendry, Miss White, and no, unfortunately, I do not have the pleasure of molding you myself."

"Aww, Mr. H., you are just too cute! You are so British!" Mary Jo squealed.

Charlie felt himself turn red. Did she have any idea how stupid she made all the Americans look?

Mr. Hendry stared intently at Mary Jo, unsure of how to respond. After a moment, he said, "Your powers of observation are slightly lacking, Ms. White. There are in fact six course leaders here at present, and if you don't mind I was just about to introduce them to you."

He glared at Mary Jo who continued to look blissfully unaware of the fact that she was making a fool of herself.

"Ooooo, I'm so sorry, Mr. H., I'm just so excited!"

"It's Mr. Hendry. Thank you, but please attempt to contain your excitement until you have quite vanished from my presence."

Mr. Hendry sighed as he continued.

"This is Dr. Robert Liston, who will be teaching Shakespearean Combat. Here we have Madame Olverna, leading Clothing and Costume; Mr. John Stuart, The Monarch and The City; Leanna Mills with Pub Culture: How Drinking Shaped the English

Countryside; Dr. Miles Richards with Propaganda: When Fact is Fiction; and finally, Dr. Arden James, leading the tutorial, Dramatizing the Unsolved History of Jack the Ripper."

Charlie sat in awe; the blonde woman was a teacher.

"All of these individuals are extremely knowledgeable in their subject areas. You are quite lucky to have the benefit of their expertise. Now for the assignments: each course advisor has a list of their students. There are twenty-six of you. With the exception of Dr. James' course, each section will have five students. Dr. James will be leading a one-on-one tutorial."

Charlie sat and listened for his name. Mary Jo—to everyone's relief—did indeed get her first choice, Clothing and Costume. Charlie hadn't put down a first choice. He had written that it didn't matter. Regardless of which class he took, his assignment was—he took a deep breath—to write a play.

The sound of complete silence shook him out of his thoughts. He looked around and realized that everyone was staring at him.

"Mr. Leder? I don't mean to wake you, but your advisor is waiting." The sarcastic tone in Mr. Hendry's voice made Charlie aware that his sluggish response was not well received.

"I'm sorry, Mr. Hendry, I was..."

"It's okay, Charlie." Arden's voice took over even as his own drifted off. "We will be staying here for the time being anyway. Please continue, Mr. Hendry."

Mr. Hendry nodded coldly and finished reading the list. Everyone drifted off to meet with their respective leaders, leaving Arden alone in the room with Charlie.

"I'm so sorry," Charlie stammered. "I didn't know you were a... um..."

"Professor? Doctor? Take your pick. Most people don't realize I am, either, so don't feel bad about it."

"But you look so young."

"Thank you. I like to think I am young. I just turned twenty-eight to be exact, and if you say I'm almost thirty, you will fail this course immediately."

Charlie laughed. "I wasn't going to say that. I'll be twenty-two in August, and it's just crazy to think of someone close to my age being a professor."

"Ah, flattery will get you everywhere. Well, I haven't been a professor for that long. In fact, I just finished my dissertation last month. But I'm done, meaning I graduated, have my doctorate, and I'm free to focus on other things."

"Such as Jack the Ripper? What exactly is the whole Jack the Ripper thing, anyway? I mean, I've heard of it. Him. It was some guy who's a famous British serial killer, but that's about all I know. Is that what you did your dissertation on?"

Arden smiled. "Well, that's about the extent of what most people know about the Ripper. Jack the Ripper is the name given to an unknown murderer from more than one hundred years ago. It's a *who*, not a *what*, although I guess the Ripper has evolved into a *what*. But to answer your other question, no. I didn't mean to focus on the Ripper in my graduate work. I actually focused on symbolism in Shakespeare. However, while I was doing that research, I accidentally came across symbols that are not only Shakespearean, but which have spanned centuries of secret organizations. I became interested. It led me to do some research that was connected to Jack the Ripper. Ripperology quickly became a hobby, and..."

"Now she's a leading Ripperologist in America," Mr. Hendry finished for her. "Dr. James, may I have a word with you? In private?" Mr. Hendry looked at Charlie as if he were an ant that needed to be squashed. It was to be expected, though. Charlie figured that Hendry probably met loads of Americans who were way too similar to Mary Jo to be nice to any of them.

Arden, however, was not about to leave her new pupil alone. "Now really isn't the best time, Richard. There is much that I need to do and I have to fill Charlie in on what's expected of him."

"Arden, it is vital that we discuss the boundaries of your present investigation. I have been meaning to discuss something with you. Yesterday evening, events occurred which might be..." He struggled with the words, not wanting to say too much in front of this young American boy. He flinched as his mind brought up the image of the butchered actress found in the streets only a few hours before. He knew that no one had told Arden about it, and that was frustrating. If she only knew what had happened, she would stop this silly idea of hers. However, he also knew her well enough to know that there would be little he could do to stop her. Arden wasn't like the silly American students who came though his programmes. She had a love for Britain that baffled him. Her passion for history, Shakespeare, and all British drama set her apart immediately. He had taken her under his wing, and when she had finally finished her work, he made sure she had a job for the fall.

However, he had not wanted Arden to conduct this course. From the beginning he had tried to dissuade her. She was adamant, however. It had been difficult for her, as an American, to gain the respect she knew she deserved as both a Shakespeare scholar and Ripperologist. When she heard that the winner of the Stafford Award was going to King's College with the sole purpose of writing a play, any play, she felt this was the job for her. It had taken some convincing on her part. She was a new professor, and an American, researching and writing about such seemingly unconnected (and such British) topics as Shakespeare and the Ripper. To most of the King's College faculty, this seemed to be an exercise in futility. Despite these setbacks, her work spoke for itself, and she managed to gain enough respect in the academic community to earn her position and guide this tutorial. There wasn't a play she thought very highly of about Jack the Ripper, and she convinced her superiors that she could write one. It would be a brilliant story when it was finished. Arden had pushed to get herself this far and wasn't going to retreat now. With her degree finally finished, she knew this was the time to focus on her career and her reputation. While she had not actually won the Stafford Award when she was at school, being in charge of this year's recipient felt pretty good.

Richard Hendry had no idea why this was so important to her. He knew her interest in the Ripper was unique; everyone knew that. However, everyone also knew that it was a hobby, and that her focus was really Shakespeare. Rumor had it she was even offered a place at Oxford. In the end, she had accepted the position at King's College. She would be teaching Shakespearean studies, and yet her summer course involved one student and a focus on Jack the Ripper. King's College would not allow her to teach any Ripperology courses, and she had not asked to. It was only this summer course. It was only this one boy, and it was only this one subject. Unable to speak about last night's murder, Mr. Richard Hendry was left powerless.

"I only hope you know what you are doing." With that he turned and left Charlie and Arden alone.

"Do you want to get out of here? There's a pub near London Bridge, one of my favorites because Shakespeare used to drink there." Arden grabbed her bag and umbrella. Charlie followed her out the door and down the windy streets.

"Why do you have an umbrella? It's not raining," Charlie asked.

"You never know around here. It's always slightly rainy. That's one thing you can count on in London. Once, I remember, I went a full month without seeing the sun."

"Man, that's crazy. Doesn't it get depressing?"

"No, not really. I like it. It's kinda cozy. Besides, I'd rather it be cold than warm. You can always add another layer, but there's only so much you can take off."

"I guess you have a point there."

Charlie started noticing the buildings as they walked out of Bankside.

"So this is South Werk?" asked Charlie.

"It's spelled South-Wark, but it's pronounced *Suthok*," Arden said. "Careful you don't pronounce it wrong or they'll start treating you like you're Mary Jo."

Charlie laughed. "Oh my Lord. Do you think she has any idea?"

"None at all. British people meet tons like her, though. I used to have a friend whose favorite game was playing with Americans. He convinced this whole tour group from some college in Kentucky that he was a direct descendant of Shakespeare. They all believed him, too. I was so embarrassed."

"We are not all like her."

"No, but a lot of the ones you meet in the tourist spots are. Or they are from New Jersey, which is a whole different source of torment. Don't get me wrong, I love being an American, but to be honest, I meet more around here that I'm embarrassed of than anything."

"How on earth do you know your way around?" Charlie was completely confused. They had only been walking for about three minutes, but they had turned about six times. None of the streets were straight, and the ones that were didn't seem to keep the same name for more than a block.

"You get used to it," she replied. "Let me give you a tour. We are right by the Globe Theatre. It's over that way. This way..."

They stopped walking for a moment at the entrance to what seemed like condominiums. There were signs detailing the history of the Globe hanging on the gated entrance. On the ground inside the parking lot were the words "THE GLOBE" arranged in a semi-circle.

"This is where the Globe actually was. They were never able to fully excavate the site, so they don't know the exact dimensions. The present Globe is based on writings, drawings, and the Rose, a Shakespeare symbol, which you can see the foundations of in that building over there."

She pointed across the street. The closed office-looking building had a separate door labeled "Rose Excavation Site."

"They excavated the site a few years ago. That's when they developed the Rose Trust. The offices were built over them, and you can see the foundations of the theatre in the basement."

"That's so weird," said Charlie. "Imagine going to work and having a five-hundred-year-old theatre in your basement."

"Yeah, the British don't get rid of things, but they don't stop building either. It's a weird mix."

They walked further along until they came to an intersection of sorts. There was an oversized brick structure directly in front of them, with a pub and the Thames on their left, and more houses to the right. Arden led him around the brick building and under an archway.

"Coming up is the Clink," Arden said. "It used to be a prison, but now it's a museum. We aren't going in there. It seems cool on the outside, but believe me, you aren't missing anything."

The grey stone building stood ominously next to a brand new restaurant.

"Look up," said Arden.

Charlie did, and was immediately disgusted by the cage hanging on the outside wall with a fake skeleton inside it.

"What is it? It looks so fake, but it's really spooky at the same time. This would scare someone in the middle of the night."

"They do that for effect," she said. "The Clink used to be one of London's most dreaded prisons. That's why if you are thrown in jail, they say you're thrown 'in the Clink.'"

A few feet past the fancy-looking restaurant, and across from a Starbucks, was a giant hole in the ground where there used to be a building.

"Okay. This is messed up." Charlie stopped walking. "A prison with a skeleton hanging outside, old brick buildings that have been converted into restaurants and Starbucks, all placed in a creepy dark alley of a street, and now there's this massive hole where a building should be? What gives? No urban planners? Why didn't they just build something here?"

Arden laughed. "This area used to be the home of the Duke of Winchester. I believe it was destroyed during World War II. I told you, they don't forget things. Rebuilding it would take away from the experience. Winchester is an interesting story anyway. Because this, Southwark, is not part of the city of London proper; that's north, across the river. Let's put it this way, there were many improper events and activities that people would leave the city for and come here. The Duke, for instance, and we're talking 15th century, kept prostitutes here who became known as the 'Winchester Geese.' Theatre didn't happen in the city either. It was considered vulgar. That's why the Globe is on the southbank. There also used to be bear baiting over here."

"What in the world is bear baiting?"

"They tied a bear to a pole and killed it. Well, they tied it to a stake and had it attacked by dogs, actually. I don't know what they found entertaining about it, but the area near the new Old Globe is called Bear Gardens."

She kept talking as they walked, pointing out different landmarks: a random sailing ship sitting in the middle of a street and St. Saviour's Church where, she noted, Shakespeare's brother is buried. Eventually they came to a main street and turned up away from the river. The street split in such a way that a labyrinth of three different strips of street seemed to grow out of a single road.

Charlie stopped walking. "Um, I don't understand this street."

Arden turned towards the right. "Don't worry, just follow me."

They walked up one of the three branches until they turned to walk through an archway that revealed an old building, set back off the main road, and benches in a large courtyard.

"This is The George. It used to surround the whole courtyard, but those two sides were bombed out during World War II. Most of the building that still stands was built in the late 1600's, but this part, where we are going, legend has it, dates back even further..."

They walked into the strangest room Charlie had ever seen, filled with the odor of old beer and cigarettes. It didn't seem to have any actual right angles. The walls and floor sloped in different directions. The furniture didn't match anything, let alone each other. The ceiling arced up and down, and the whole room curved precariously as if it was being held together by sheer will.

"I love this room. It's so wonky," Arden commented.

"Yeah," said Charlie, "that's a word for it."

Arden went for drinks while Charlie looked around. There was a cellar door in one corner, a fireplace in another, and a pathway, to what he assumed was the rest of the pub, near the front. It was interesting and all, but his mind drifted back to Arden. She was captivating, and he loved how everything in London seemed to interest her. It somehow made him want to know more about the city. He carefully examined the room, fishing for questions to ask when she returned.

"Here you go. I hope you like good British beer. I also got you a soda just in case."

Charlie nodded and took a sip of the warm beer. After a minute, he decided to go with the soda. It was still a bit early for beer.

"Okay, so now is when I tell you what you will be doing for the next few weeks. To start with, how much detail exactly do you know about Jack the Ripper?"

Charlie looked at her in confusion. "Well, not much. He was a serial killer in London. That's about it."

"Yep. The one-sentence version is he was someone or ones who killed prostitutes in the slums of Victorian London."

"They never caught him or them, did they?"

"Exactly, they never did. It's one of the greatest unsolved mysteries ever."

Charlie thought for a moment. "You know, this is cool and all. I mean, don't get me wrong, I'm really interested, but I have this assignment while I'm here. I have to..."

"Write a play."

Charlie was surprised. "Yeah, you know."

"I know, that's where I come in, actually. I'm writing it with you. Or rather, we are writing it together. We'll produce it at the end of the summer with actors from the summer school. You know, you might even get to direct it."

Charlie had no idea everything was already organized. "Wow, you really are ready for me. Listen, to be perfectly honest, I haven't really been that excited about coming here, and I guess I haven't paid as much attention to all that's been planned as I should have."

"Not excited? Why not? Wait. Hold that thought. You'll tell me later. Let's put anything that you are not excited about behind us. You'll enjoy it, I promise. I'll fill you in on the Ripper, and then I'll make you love London and never want to go home."

"Well, I don't know that I'd go that far."

"How far?"

"The 'love London' thing. I mean, I wouldn't mind being distracted. I welcome distraction, actually. But I'm not sure about the never wanting to go home part. I'm already looking forward to going home. I miss it."

Arden laughed. "You sound like Dorothy at the end of *The Wizard of Oz*. 'There's no place like home, there's no place like home.'"

Charlie smiled through his embarrassment. "Okay, so I'm a big baby."

"I think I'll keep you around anyway," Arden replied, smiling at him.

Charlie stared, feeling her smile penetrate through his hesitations. Finally, he was able to speak again.

"Let me get this straight. We are writing a play together based on your research? That's the course?"

"Yep. That's about it."

"Do I have any choice in the matter?"

"Not particularly."

"Out of curiosity, why me?" Charlie shrugged.

"I... Well, let me start from the beginning. I was excited about the prospect of writing a play about the Ripper. Like you, I have always been a theatre person, and I tend to put my research into my plays. Usually I work alone, but this year I haven't really had any free time. When I got the King's job, I realized I had a great opportunity. I also thought it would be a good idea to give back in a way. I went to undergrad at your school, so I figured when the Stafford recipient was announced, I would see what they were thinking of doing in the hopes of drafting them.

"When we put out the literature for this program, lots of people applied because they had heard about the work we were doing and wanted to be a part of it. However, that's dangerous because I didn't want any wild theories or preconceived notions clouding the truth. That's what I am after, of course, the truth. I have been for a while. There are loads of Ripperologists floating about. All of them have their own ideas about who Jack the Ripper was. Many people like to pretend to be Perry Mason or something and come to this field determined to be the hero. You see the titles of some of their books—*Jack the Ripper, Case Closed* or *Jack the Ripper, the Final Solution*."

"Are any of them, right?" Charlie asked.

"They might be. They might have parts that are right, or there might not *be* a right. That's what's hard for people to understand. There are more questions the deeper you look. Nearly every answer is a question. Jack the Ripper is responsible for as few as five and as many as seven, or even more murders. That is to say, there are many murders that occurred in 1888 and 1889, but five of them were undisputedly committed by the same person—the Ripper. Those are what I'm focusing on. I don't care to look at things that are irrelevant. It's like looking at Shakespeare's plays and focusing on who wrote them. Whether Shakespeare was Shakespeare is irrelevant. It only distracts from the point."

"And that point is..." Charlie found himself intrigued.

"That we probably have been talking about the real killer the whole time. That all these theories have bits to them that are true, and parts of them that are conjecture. What people think tends to cloud the picture. Stephen Knight, for instance, wrote a book where he said the Masons were behind the Ripper murders. Knight hated the Masons. He wrote books condemning them. Those books aren't even accurate. He is part of the lore that says the Freemasons began as the stonemason guilds of the Middle Ages. They didn't, though; it's been proven since Knight's book came out that they evolved from a branch of soldier monks called the Templar Knights. However, to look at that would have destroyed some of his anti-Masonic stance, so he chose to ignore it. Too many people choose to ignore valid theories because they interfere with their own biased viewpoints."

"Maybe I've been living in a theatre for too long, but to say I'm confused is an understatement," Charlie interjected. "So, let's start with this: if there were other murders, why is the Ripper important? Why is he called the Ripper?"

"The Ripper is called that because he didn't just kill the girls, he mutilated them. He strangled them, cut their throats, ripped them open, ripped out and stole their organs, and in some cases practically disassembled them. Especially in the case of his last victim, Mary Kelly, where he pretty much dissected her. He didn't just kill. He ripped."

"He ripped them open and stole their organs," Charlie repeated.

"Yes. It's not just that it's unsolved; it's that it is so gruesome and unsolved. Each of the five wasn't just killed. They were desecrated—something which didn't happen all that often in the dimly lit and relatively highly traveled streets of Victorian London."

"Huh. And the Masons..."

"I'll get back to that later. I'm sorry, tangent because of a theory."

"Okay, now, all this is interesting, but I still don't understand one fundamental thing."

"Which is?"

"What does this have to do with the play? Is this what we are writing about?" Charlie was hooked, but he was also confused. Was he going to be spending the summer solving an unsolved mystery as well as writing a play about it?

As if she was reading his mind, Arden laughed and shook her head. "I'm sorry, I'm getting off track. You are not going to solve the Ripper murders. At least I don't think you will. If you do, let me know—it would save me a ton of work. The murders took place quite near here, in the Whitechapel district. One took place in the actual City district. Both areas are across the river."

"Wait a second. If we're not trying to solve the Ripper murders, then what is the play about?"

"I'm getting to that. See, last year I published a book about Jack the Ripper. One that put many existing theories together to create a more logical progression. I didn't solve the case, but I did present a new theory. My theory is quite controversial, and although it does not involve any organization as a whole, it is a bit of a conspiracy theory. As I said, we'll be writing, producing, and directing a play. We are going to take my theory, and together create a piece that puts the specifics of my theory into a visual form. Without solving the crime, my book simply suggests motives. I take other suspects and show who could have been involved. This is why it's controversial. I challenge theories that could not be correct. I point out inconsistencies, and I show what type of person, or rather, people came together to be 'the Ripper.'"

"You know that all I know is what you just told me."

Arden nodded. "I'm glad you don't have preconceived notions about this subject, and as a theatre major, you are the perfect person to help put it into visual language."

"Sounds like a plan," Charlie shrugged.

"Good. I'm glad you agree."

"You'll have to tell me a little more about this theory of yours, though."

"Don't worry about that yet. Before we start writing, I am determined to show you around the whole of London, the Ripper part of London, the theatre scene, and then we'll get to work."

"Do you think we'll be able to do all that, write this thing, and produce it in the eight weeks I have here? I do leave at the end of the summer," Charlie reminded his professor.

"Absolutely. I've spaced it out. We'll only spend a day or two wandering around, I promise. You cannot possibly be any help to me until you've seen this city. Or until you appreciate how incredibly easy it is to see shows around here."

"Shows? Which ones? How much do they cost?" Charlie loved seeing live theatre but was so busy—and poor—that he barely had any time to do so.

"All of them. Any of them. There are concessions, half-price tickets, you name it. It is so simple to see theatre here." Arden stood up and put on her jacket. "Are you ready?"

Charlie looked intently at the woman standing across from him. He felt himself grow more comfortable despite this strange scenario. He didn't know her, but somehow, he trusted her.

Charlie smiled. "Well, I guess we'd better get started."

## Chapter 5

**"Misery acquaints a man with strange bedfellows." – *The Tempest***

Outside the pub, Peter looked at his watch. It was early in the day, but he felt like it was much later. It had been a really long night and it was raining again. That girl, he sighed, and the same dream. He shook his head.

"I need a pint," he heard himself say. He looked through the glass. They weren't moving; there would be plenty of time for just one pint. Besides, despite his huge hat, which he was using as a disguise, he was getting soaked. He had thought about going inside the small room, but he knew she'd recognize him. Besides, she was wearing the pin. He could hear her. She had loved that pin, and thankfully remained blissfully unaware that it held a tiny video/audio device. With her sitting, casually facing the kid, the audio was all that he really needed for the time being. As he started towards the part of The George where the actual bar was, his mobile rang.

"Bloody 'ell," he said, answering it. "'Ello, Gov. What's the news?"

"Where is she?" the voice at the other end of the line asked.

"In a pub. She's got her student now. They're chattin' 'bout the Ripper. Makin' plans, that sort of thing."

"Let me know if anything changes. Don't forget, her book was there."

"Yep, I know. Looks like they're gettin' up now and headin' out. I'll ring you back if anythink 'appens."

He hung up the phone and watched as Charlie and Arden walked out of The George.

Holding the earpiece back to his ear, Peter listened intently to Arden's voice.

"And then they found Mary Kelly. She was the last one. There were other murders that have since been suggested to be Ripper murders, but there is no proof. At the time, well, shortly after, they suddenly closed the case, calling it unsolved. That's what is the strangest thing to me.

"Am I supposed to comment on that?" Charlie asked.

Arden laughed. "No, don't worry about it."

Peter smiled to himself. All her questions. She used to ask him all the time. Not for real, of course. He would get home while she was writing, and she would bombard him with questions. He knew that was why he was there. Or at least why he had been there at first. All those pretty birds out there, and here was one with her nose in a book or computer. Tons of girls fancied him. He'd walk into a club and they'd all look. He never spent any money 'cause the birds paid for it all. Sexy girls. Girls out to have a good time. Not serious ones like her.

When he was learning about the assignment, it had sounded so good. Pick up some girl, get her to trust you, keep an eye on her, pretend to be homeless, move in, learn even more. They had shown him a picture. She was a looker, so he'd gone along with it. It took about a day before he was sorry.

Peter stopped walking and turned towards the water. Yeah, he'd been sorry, at first. But then… She was so different than all those other girls. She knew so much. And took care of things and was responsible. And she had made his nightmares go away.

Chapter 6

**"What's in a name? That which we call a rose By any other name would smell as sweet."**

***– Romeo and Juliet***

Arden lay in bed that night, her mind racing back over everything she had done during the day. It had been amazing. They had walked all over London. She showed him all the tourist sites, or rather they had passed through all the tourist sites. Westminster Abbey, Parliament, the Tower of London, Buckingham Palace... She exhausted Charlie. By evening, he was ready to call it a day. They grabbed dinner, and she took him to see his first West End show, The Reduced Shakespeare Company's *The Complete Works of William Shakespeare, Abridged*.

"That was the funniest thing I have ever seen in my life," Charlie had said as they were leaving the theatre.

"Good introduction to British theatre?"

"Awesome. And the tickets were so cheap!"

"Concessions. Ten pounds an hour before the show."

"It was all improv."

"Not really. There is a script. I actually have it, but they do different improv stuff every show. It's good but that's what makes it even better."

"That's what makes it incredible. I love improv. I love doing improv, too. I was watching and found myself wanting to jump up onstage and act alongside them."

"Are you an actor, too? I thought you just did production, tech—you know, backstage work."

"Yeah. I do it all." He cleared his throat and puffed out his chest. "I'm your atypical triple threat: acting, producing, stage managing" he laughed at himself, "but really, I love doing improv. We have an improv troupe at my school—"

"The Rude Mechanicals. I went there, too, remember?"

"Oh yeah. You told me that. What was it like? Did you do theatre?"

"Yep. I did forty-one shows while I was there. I stage-managed a ton, designed lights, ran sound and light boards, directed three, and all the while was Production Manager. Talk about being a threat; at one point, anyone who wanted to even audition for any show had to talk to me."

"Wait a second." Charlie thought. "Arden James. Oh my God. I do know who you are. You were the first student to be Production Manager. You graduated the year before I started."

"Yeah, wow, I'm impressed."

"You used to have parties at your house every weekend."

"Yeah, I did. They were crazy. We always had about a million people over. We tried to get creative, too. We always came up with fun themes and games. I loved it there."

"Do you miss it?" Charlie asked.

"I do, but I don't. If I had to create my perfect world, all the people I went to school with would be there. However, I can't do that, and I've moved on. Granted, I'm not always sure what I've moved on *to*, but I'm not the same person I was at school. None of my friends are either. We all have grown up."

"I understand," Charlie nodded.

"You do?"

"Yes. I mean, I've had a great time, and I loved it there, but I feel like... I don't know, like I've done everything there is to do there. I'm looking for something new. Something different. I don't know. I'll find it eventually."

Arden yawned. "Well, we're here, anyway. At your building."

Charlie nodded. "Thank you for a really fun day."

Arden smiled to herself. It had been a while since she had really just relaxed and had fun. Charlie made her laugh. It was nice to be with someone like that again.

She turned over and started to drift off to sleep when her phone rang. Groggily, she picked it up.

"Hello?"

"Ms. James, I presume."

"Who may I say is calling?"

"This is Detective Andrews with the Metropolitan police. I am sorry to disturb you so late in the evening, but it is my unfortunate duty to inform you that you are in extreme danger. I am afraid that although I am indisposed, you must come to Scotland Yard immediately. My deputy will explain. I will see you later. A car will be there in five minutes. Goodnight."

Arden stared at the phone in confusion. The sound of the doorbell surprised her out of her trance.

"I'll be one minute," she yelled, and got dressed as fast as she could before heading downstairs and getting into the police car.

Chapter 7

**"My troublous dreams this night doth make me sad." – *Henry VI part II***

At breakfast the next day, Charlie looked for Arden. He was ready for another day of traipsing about the city. She was going to show him all the actual Ripper sites today. He didn't see her, so after breakfast he sat on a bench outside and waited.

Arden finally showed up looking tired and somewhat strained. She also looked anxious.

"I'm sorry I'm late," she said, peering around.

"It's okay; where are we going now?"

"Well, there's been something..." Arden scanned around again. "Let's get out of here. We have to talk." She took him back to The George, which would be deserted at this hour, and ordered a large coffee.

"The plan was to explore different Ripper sites, but well, something's happened."

Her voice trailed off and the silence of the empty room gave Charlie a strange, uncomfortable feeling.

"Last night I received a call. From the police. It seems," she continued, clearing her throat and lowering her voice, "a girl was killed. She was found in the exact same place as the first Ripper victim—Mary Nichols. She was killed the same way".

"The same way?"

"As the first Ripper victim of the five. She was found in Buck's Row, Whitechapel. She had been strangled, her throat had been cut and she was disemboweled."

"That's disgusting," Charlie grimaced.

"Charlie, this is top-secret information. No one knows yet. It hasn't even been in the papers."

"How do you know then?" Charlie was beginning to worry.

"I know because the police contacted me. There was something at the crime scene which made it necessary for the police to involve me in the investigation. That's why Richard Hendry didn't want me to continue with this course. He knew about it yesterday but didn't want to tell me. He thinks it will be too dangerous to continue and feels that I should turn your seminar into something to do only with Shakespeare."

Charlie sat still for a moment. "Are you going to?"

"Charlie, I have spent so much time in the last few years studying the Ripper. I want to do the right thing, but it's more vital now than ever that the truth comes out. I know this is only one girl, but if the old Ripper crimes are being copied, there could be at least four more murders. I don't know why anything involving me would have been there, but I know that it forces me to be involved. I don't expect you to solve the mystery of 1888. I don't really expect to solve it myself any more than I already think I have. But I must have touched a nerve with someone. I think I've been doing something that someone doesn't want me to do. I can't just stop or not get involved. I need to find the truth. Look, you don't need to get involved in this. I can have you go work with one of the other professors. Many of the courses are about theatre or some aspect of theatre. You can write your play about something else."

"What the hell is going on? Arden?" Charlie took a deep breath. "Look, I just met you. I don't know what's going on. But the fact is, I like you. I had fun yesterday. I want to work with you. I really didn't have any interest in coming here, and now I can't wait to get started. Whatever you have to do, well, I want to help."

"Do you mean that?" she asked instinctively. Arden looked deep into his eyes. There was something about them — an honesty. She wanted him to help her but knew she couldn't force him into anything.

She turned away. "No. I don't want you to. It might get dangerous."

"Screw that. I like dangerous. It's fun." Anytime anyone told Charlie not to do something, it just made him want to do it even more. Charlie was not going to be pushed away. He wanted to help her and that was that.

Arden didn't respond. She stared down at the floor again, becoming focused to the point of distraction. Charlie broke her reverie to urge her on.

"Come on, tell me. What was found at the crime scene?" Charlie demanded, determined.

Arden's gaze slowly shifted from the uneven wood planks up towards him. She looked long and hard into his eyes before finally answering the question.

"That's what's so strange," she said. "My book."

"Your Ripper book?"

"No," she said, "a copy of my dissertation, *Symbolism in Shakespeare*."

## Chapter 8

**"Tomorrow, and tomorrow, and tomorrow, Creeps in this petty pace from day to day,"**

**- *Macbeth***

Neither of them said anything for a few moments. Charlie needed to process all he just heard. He was in a foreign country, on a course he had thought, until yesterday, would only get as exciting as dealing with uppity British actors. Now he was suddenly thrust into some strange, macabre investigation. He didn't know what to think.

His mind floated back to the final straw, the trigger that convinced him to leave home and college: Cassie had dumped him. His girlfriend of two years had first cheated on him and then dumped him. He hadn't wanted to leave her. They had even talked about her travelling to England with him. Then he had come home early from rehearsal and there she was, with the lead actor in the last play he just directed. She had even whined about having to see the show, but apparently at the cast party the two hit it off. It was the stuff of B-rated vaudeville: every night when Charlie left for rehearsal, Cassie snuck Martin into their house. It had been too much. Charlie had even started picking out an engagement ring. And then this. Without a second thought he left the house and eventually the country; and almost all feeling had left him.

Now he was in a strange bar with a strange woman who was telling him that she was suddenly involved in a murder investigation. For the first time in a while, Charlie actually started to feel something; he felt...excitement.

"How can I help?" he asked. "Or rather, what should we do? Surely there are at least a thousand people who know as much as you about the Ripper murders. At least a thousand. You said so yourself."

"That is exactly what I need to find out," she sighed.

"Well, what should I do first? I mean, I could walk into Scotland Yard and say, 'Hi, my name is Charlie Leder, and I'm here to solve a murder,' but I don't think they'd buy it." He stared at her intently.

"Okay, you can stay," she finally said.

"Thank you."

"But seriously, keep an eye out, and be careful. Already, I think I'm being followed."

"What makes you think that?"

"I don't know, just this feeling I have. Maybe I'm going crazy, but I feel like someone is looking for me to do something. As soon as I do, who knows what will happen. There are still four more murders that would follow the Ripper pattern if I, or I guess *we*, don't do something, and fast. If you want out, you just have to say. Please say now though, 'cause if you wait, it may be too late. I only ask that you don't say a word to anyone about this. Please, Charlie, think about this before you stay."

A few moments of silence followed as Charlie thought about the situation. Something about it intrigued him, and something about Arden made him want to stay with her. He took a long look at her. This intelligent, confident, older woman looked both fierce and vulnerable. He wanted to drink in her every word as much as he wanted to protect her from whatever danger lurked. As he searched her face to understand the dichotomy, her brown eyes, widened with fear and anticipation, met his gaze. He took her hand from across the table, which surprised her as much as it did him, but she didn't resist or pull away.

"No. I already said I wanted to stay, and I do. I'll stay. At least it won't be a boring summer, right?"

"That's for sure. And I promise as soon as we are done, we will get back to what we were supposed to do in the first place. Maybe this will inspire you to write a better play, right?"

"The play. I was trying to forget about that." He let his grip loosen and she pulled her hand away.

"Why?"

"I'm just not really looking forward to that part. I've never written a play before." He stopped for a second and thought about things he had written. "I've written songs, but they are really short compared to plays."

"You've written songs?" The news caught Arden by surprise. "That's awesome. I'd like to hear one sometime."

"Get me a guitar and I'll play one for you whenever you like."

"Maybe I will," she smiled. "Don't worry about writing a play. I'll be there to help every step of the way."

He smiled back. "And so will I. Anyway, this mystery of yours. Where do we start?"

"Where else? The theatre."

They rose and headed out, into the grey but thankfully dry London streets. Once again, a few steps behind trailed Peter, this time wearing a fake beard and baseball cap. He put down his just-pulled pint and looked longingly at his glass.

"Blast," he said, and followed them out the door.

## Chapter 9

**"All the world's a stage, And all the men and women merely players;**

**They have their exits and their entrances, And one man in his time plays many parts" -**

***As You Like It***

The new Globe stage was beautiful. Charlie had never seen anything like it. In re-constructing the 16th-century structure, the builders used materials that were as authentic to Shakespeare's time as possible. They kept as close as possible to the original design or at least what they decided was the original design. The result was an awe-inspiring building seemingly pulled right out of Elizabethan England. It even smelled old. It was round and made of wood. Arden said the kind of wood used was known as "green" oak, an oak that was felled in the last 18 months and therefore had relatively high moisture content: typically, 60-80%. It was used in the 16th century because it was strong, durable and much easier than seasoned oak to cut and shape precisely, which was crucial for a round structure. The stage was deep and wide, and it jutted out into the center of the circle. There was an extensively broad space where the groundlings would have stood to watch the show, and there were three tiers of seating in the structure itself. Two massive pillars on each side of the stage held up the partial roof that covered the stage and seats, but the groundlings' section, where theatre goers stood on the ground, was completely exposed. Cheaper than the cheap seats, inclement weather was the price you paid.

The stage was painted in an ornate and almost overly decorative manner. The ceiling above the stage had the complete cycle of the Zodiac, and the remainder of the space was covered with an almost overwhelming array of differing geometric, opulent, and unique patterns. Each was painted with a careful attention to detail. Nearly every color of the rainbow was represented. These decorations imbued the entire space with the feel of a pulsing energy.

"And an American was responsible for this?" he asked. Though still reeling from his new role as detective, the theatre person in him was captivated by the story of the Globe Theatre.

"Yes, an American actor, Sam Wanamaker. He came here over fifty years ago looking for some monument to the old Globe, and when he found only a commemorative plaque, he immediately decided to rebuild it. Unfortunately, he died before it was finished. His daughter continued his dream until it reached completion. It was only finished a few years ago. I've been involved in the education department of the Globe since its second season, and I've fallen in love with it." She smiled. "I'm glad you like it so much."

"I would love to work in this space."

"You might get that chance. However, we have other work to do now."

"Why are we here again?" Charlie asked, forcing himself to stop staring at the stage.

"Well, there are very few people who have copies of my dissertation. My copy is still at home, and I doubt my parents or grandparents flew a copy over from America for it to be placed at a crime scene. My advisor still has his; I checked this morning. Since we are looking for missing hard copies, the only other option is here. Because it was about Shakespeare, and I worked with Globe researchers, I gave the Education Department three copies. The Director of Education, Winston Patrick, loved it and wanted to publish it so that it could be sold and used in some of the courses. That hasn't happened yet. It's still in the works. To be honest, I'm not really sure what the holdup has been. It's been done for a while, and Winston assured me that it's been submitted to a publisher who has accepted it. Anyway, the copy found at the crime scene was one of the ones that I had printed myself, so as I said, this is the only place left where one could be missing."

It seemed to make sense, as much sense as anything made to Charlie at that moment. Maybe he was still jetlagged and this was all part of a really strange dream. However, as Charlie chased Arden around the backstage corridors of the Globe, the reality of the situation became unavoidable. They finally arrived at an office, which smelled like after-shave and whisky. A straggly man with thick dark hair was hovering behind a desk full of medieval, stunted-looking figurines.

"Winston? Winston, I've brought a friend from the States who's been dying to meet you. Umm, Winston? What are those?" asked Arden, stopping short at the sight of the figurines.

"A chess board. Or rather, chess pieces. *Richard III*. I don't know if this concept will quite translate, but the director is insistent, and what is worse, he doesn't trust our prop master. Can you imagine? I told him they would be perfectly safe, but as these are irreplaceable items of deep sentimental importance, the crazy fool felt they needed to live in my office. What on earth am I going to do with a table full of hideously ugly chess pieces?" Winston Patrick didn't look up or acknowledge Charlie in any way. However, Charlie thought, if I had a table full of demented Hobbit-like statues, I don't think I would care too much about some college kid standing in my doorway.

"Why doesn't he trust the prop master?" Charlie whispered. "Is the guy really weird or something? We once had this one jerkoff doing props for us who became really attached to this fake gun for one show. We practically had to tie the guy up so we could return it to the rental place. He cried for a week. Some people take their jobs way too seriously." Charlie started laughing to himself, at which point he finally noticed the disapproving stares coming from both Arden and Winston.

"Yes, well, anyway," Winston disregarded Charlie and spoke directly to Arden. "What can I do for you?"

"It's a long story, but I sent my parents my dissertation, and my advisor isn't in town at the moment, and Charlie here really wanted to see it. I gave you a few copies and wanted to know if I could borrow one for a bit."

"Of course. Let me see. There's the one in the shop; we wouldn't want to take that one. I have one at home, but the third copy is here in the office. Let me see."

As Winston started looking around, Charlie's eyes wandered around the whole room. It was an interesting space. It was quite large, with a second desk placed at the other side of the room. There were three overflowing bookcases covering the back wall, and all other wall space was filled with Shakespeare posters: *Macbeth, Two Gentlemen of Verona, The Tempest, Henry V, Romeo and Juliet*. Nearly half of Shakespeare's plays were represented. He walked over and stared inquisitively at *The Tempest* poster. It was one of the most interesting ones he had ever seen. Having just done a lighting design project for *The Tempest*, he was moderately familiar with the show. The poster was a mass of color with Prospero at the center. Prospero was standing on the Globe stage, but he was twice as big as the stage. The whole poster seemed to move with a steady symmetry. The floor of the stage was black and white but rich, vibrant reds, greens, blues, and yellows swirled in a diamond shape around Prospero. In the corner he noticed a handwritten number.

"Huh," he heard himself say, "Limited Edition."

He paused for a moment. That's strange, he thought. It looks like a typical publicity poster. He didn't know there were limited editions of publicity posters.

He was so fascinated by the poster that it took him a while to realize another person had come in. A snooty-looking, lanky man with small, geeky wire-framed glasses was standing awkwardly behind Charlie. As Charlie took a step back to get a better look at the poster, he accidentally stepped on the stranger's foot.

"I'm sorry," Charlie said, feeling embarrassed. "I didn't see you."

"Do you like *The Tempest*?" The stranger's eyes stared intensely down at Charlie from behind the spectacles.

"Umm, I just did a project, at school. Lighting design on *The Tempest*. It was awesome. For the storm I had a cyc that was lit with these rotating gobos, and had more gobos focused down on the stage, which I covered with these awesome new fog machines—"

"Alec, there you are," Winston interrupted before Alec could comment on the young brash American's boast of theatre jargon. "Have you seen my copy of Arden's dissertation?"

Alec turned towards the others.

"No, I don't recall that I have. Which dissertation was that again? We have so many books; it's hard to remember one from another."

Charlie could feel Arden bristle from the other side of the room.

"It was the one about Shakespeare and symbolism. Come on Alec, you know the one. We put a copy in the shop."

"Well then you know where it is."

"No, I had one here, as well. I know I kept one copy on my desk."

"Winston, old boy, you have about five hundred books in this room. I'm sure it's here somewhere."

"I'm sure it's not. I hadn't put it away yet."

"Have you checked the lounge? Maybe you brought it in there. All these Shakespeare buffs around. I'm sure someone just picked it up. Shakespeare, secret societies, medieval lore, faeries; that's what gets these blokes off."

"So you've read it, Alec," It took a minute for Arden to neutralize the suspicious glare from her face. She sensed he had seen it and was beginning to suspect there was little doubt that Alec knew the location of her manuscript.

"As I stated clearly before, we get a large number of texts delivered to us. I don't often recall one over another."

"Thank you. I understand. I thought it sounded for a moment like you had read it."

Arden turned to Charlie. "Well, I'm really sorry; I guess you'll just have to wait to read it. I know how disappointed you are."

Without missing a beat, Charlie replied, "Hey, I understand, but what am I going to tell my professor? This whole scholarship was given to me on the basis that I had this friend that had written this great book. I was supposed to use it to do my project. I have no idea what I'll do now."

"Scholarship?" Winston's eyes brightened a bit at that. "What scholarship?"

"There's this award they give out at college. It's a scholarship which requires you to do theatre in London. I have to write a play as part of my award. I was so totally looking forward to writing a... a... symbolic piece on um, well, Shakespeare. I loved doing the..." Charlie looked frantically around the office for clues. "*Tempest*. *The Tempest*, the lighting design project, so I wanted to do more with Shakespeare. Maybe, you know, faeries and all that. Well, I hadn't thought it through yet, but the dissertation was important."

Arden was impressed by Charlie's ability to improvise based on the limited information he had been given. She was about to say as much when Alec caught her eye. There was something about his icy stare that made her feel uneasy.

"I see." Alec had the most condescending voice Charlie had ever heard. "Whatever you end up writing, I can tell there will be no shortage of dialogue," Alec snorted as he pushed the wire frames of his glasses firmly towards his beady eyes.
He turned away from Charlie as if there was no need to have anything else to do with this silly American child. "Winston, I just came by to tell you I was leaving for the day. I have a family emergency and must hurry off to attend to it. If you need me, I will be on my mobile."

"I'm so sorry to hear that. I do hope it's nothing too terrible."

"Thank you." With that, Alec slithered out of the room as silently as he had entered.

"We must be going, as well." Arden took Charlie's arm and pulled him away from his corner near *The Tempest* poster. "I do thank you for looking, Winston."

"Well, now, I just might have a solution. We can take the book from the shop for a short time. That way you will have no trouble getting started on your project, young man."

Charlie could see the urgency in Arden's eyes, but she reluctantly followed Winston down to the gift shop. It took a while to descend the seemingly endless flights of stairs as Winston refused to take the elevator. He also insisted on taking the long way round. Winston was not an old man, but he was no youngster. He walked with a pronounced limp. It was clear to Charlie that at a minimum, exhaustion had taken over. Either that or Winston had no concept of time and distance. It would have taken them about two minutes to get to the bookstore had they used the elevator. However, taking the stairs and the long way, including a swing around to the back of the Globe stage and crossing through the groundlings' space to the outer door, caused this journey to last about a half hour. Upon entering the shop, Winston marched over to a display case. Charlie peered inside but didn't see anything.

"What are we looking at?" he asked.

"Nothing..." Arden sucked her breath in disbelief as she spoke the words. "It's gone, too."

The woman behind the shop counter came over to them. "Winston? Is there something I can help you with, luv?"

"The manuscript that was here... There was that book that we had put on display as pre-publicity for the widespread publication."

"Yes, I remember. There have been many compliments on it. I told Alec when he borrowed it that we didn't want it gone for too long now. Our Molly has already ordered three copies, and there's not been one teacher here yet that hasn't wanted to have a look at it."

"Alec? He borrowed it? When?" Arden looked as pale as a ghost.

"Why, just a bit ago, dearie. He was in quite the hurry. Said he needed it right away. I unlocked the case, he took it, and off he went."

"A few minutes ago?" Charlie asked. Damn the stairs. They would have probably bumped into him if they hadn't spent years going about thirty feet.

Winston looked deeply confused. "Why did he want it?"

"Well, Winston, luv, he said you needed him to take a copy right off to the British Library. I didn't ask why, I thought that Winston knows his own mind. I didn't fancy you didn't have your own copy."

"I didn't. This is madness. Let me know the moment he brings it back. Imagine, using me as an excuse to steal this young lady's work. Thank you for all your help. We must be going."

The woman behind the counter also looked confused but nodded in reply.

Winston turned toward Arden. "I think we'd better go back up to my office."

"Actually Winston, do you mind taking a walk? I find myself suddenly in need of fresh air."

**Chapter 10**

**"Lord, what fools these mortals be!" -*Midsummer Night's Dream***

Peter hated Alec. He was such a pansy-ass wanker. Alec had been far too easy to manipulate. Even listening to his weaselly, screechy voice on the earpiece hurt. Peter stood up and stretched. Looking around, he noticed a group of giggly uni-type girls in short jean skirts standing in front of the Globe with cameras.

"'Merican Tourists," he snickered. "Far too easy. And I do seem to 'ave some time on me hands."

Peter walked over to the girls who had stopped taking pictures and were now examining a map.

"'Ello, ladies. You all right? How can I help?"

"OOOOOHHHHH My G-d! You're British, aren't you?!" screamed Mary Jo.

Taking a minute to regain his hearing, Peter simply nodded.

"You have the sexiest accent in the whole wide world! Oh, I just want to wrap you up and give you for Christmas!"

The drawl and volume pierced Peter's ear drums. Thankfully a momentary lull in her screeching allowed Peter to hear Arden's voice in his earpiece. They were coming outside. Blast, he thought. It's been forever since I pulled. This one's a pain, but at least she's easy.

Peter reached his hand nonchalantly into his pocket, felt for his phone, and hit the ringtone key. The loud mobile phone ring thankfully released him from her grasp. He made his apologies, assured her that he would be back in a moment, and seeing Arden and friends emerge from the Globe, directed Mary Jo to a coffee place in the opposite direction. There would be time for that later.

## Chapter 11

**"Life's but a walking shadow, a poor player, That struts and frets his hour upon the stage, And then is heard no more. It is a tale Told by an idiot, full of sound and fury, Signifying nothing." - *Macbeth***

Charlie, Arden, and Winston walked along the boardwalk in silence until they hit Blackfriars Bridge. Arden stopped first and sat down on a convenient bench.

"Well, Arden," Winston exhaled. "Are you ready to tell me what the hell is going on around here? You, boy. You don't need to write a play, do you?"

"Actually I..."

"He does, but that's not important, Winston. The other night someone was murdered."

"Murdered?"

"Yes. In the style of Jack the Ripper."

"I'm terribly sorry to hear that, but I'm sure that has nothing to do with us here at the Globe."

"Unfortunately, it does. My dissertation was at the scene."

"The one I read?"

Arden nodded. "Yes. That's why I needed to know where all the existing copies were. I now know about the one from your desk, but it scares me to think where the shop copy is going to end up."

Winston thought for a minute. “And you’re sure that all the other copies are accounted for?”

“Yes, positive. I mean, at least the ones I made. I guess if someone had one copy, they could Xerox... they could make any number of additional copies. Wow, who knows how many could be floating around. But why would Alec want the store copy? And for that matter, what in the world could my book have been doing at the murder site?”

“My, my. This is a sticky situation,” Winston concluded.

“That’s an understatement,” murmured Charlie.

Silence filled the air as the trio became lost in thought. Arden’s mind drifted across the familiar scene of the Thames River. It was so beautiful. So peaceful. Her eyes wandered past St. Paul’s Cathedral to the mouth of London Bridge. As they did, her thoughts traveled back to Shakespeare.

“Hey, Charlie,” Arden said as she stared across the river. “Here’s more London trivia for you. London Bridge used to have all kinds of houses on it. It was the only bridge at the time and would get really crowded. People used to take boats to get across the Thames. The river acted as one city border, and there was a wall that went around the rest of the city. This wall had gates,” she said as she stared across the Thames at Blackfriars train station. “There used to be a gatehouse over there. Blackfriars Gatehouse. That area was filled with secret passageways where they used to smuggle papists and Catholic priests. Shakespeare purchased the top floor of the gatehouse in 1613.”

"One of the bigger mysteries of the Bard's life actually," Winston added. "He was living primarily in Stratford by then, so no one knows why he would have wanted to buy land in London. It wasn't quite so easy to get around as it is today. Now it is only a ninety-mile train ride that one must take to get from Stratford to London if Shakespeare were to check on his purchase. At the time, it would have been a much more rigorous journey. And what makes it even more mysterious is he sold the property almost immediately after buying it. And no one knows why."

Charlie was too busy organizing the mass of newly acquired Ripper information to turn his attention to something so off topic as Shakespeare's land holdings.

He turned to Arden, "Who was the first Ripper victim? How was she killed again?"

"Well, the first murder that is incontrovertibly the Ripper is Mary Anne, or Polly, Nichols. She was found with her throat sliced left to right, so deeply that it cut through her windpipe, spinal cord, and vocal cords. She was ripped open, or her stomach was, exposing her intestines. This was on August 31, 1888, in a yard crossing what was called Buck's Row in Whitechapel. She was a prostitute who had 'fallen into drink,' as they say. Basically, she had no real money, no real home, and lived from day to day on the streets. She was boarding in a house near where she was found and had ventured out in the middle of the night to get money for her bed. Several people had seen her around the area earlier in the day. She was found between three and four in the morning."

"Is that place, Buck's Row or whatever; is that near here?"

"Not far, actually."

"It still exists?"

"Oh yes. London has grown exponentially, but the actual city itself really hasn't changed that much in the past five centuries. Not like things change in America. Here, the area still exists even if buildings have changed. In the case of Nichols, the place where she was found is close to its original form. There's a wall now where the gate was that she had been lying next to, but the spot is still there. It's where they found the girl the other night, remember? Same spot, same wounds."

"And you said there were five people killed?"

"Yes. Five agreed-upon Ripper victims."

"Who was the second one?"

"Annie Chapman. She was also a prostitute. She was found in the yard of number 29 Hanbury Street, Spitalfields, on September 8, 1888."

"What happened to her?"

"She had the same throat wounds, but in addition to ripping open her abdomen, he removed a few internal organs as well."

Even as she said the words, Arden had a sickening feeling creep through her body. "It's too soon, though. Nine days separated the first two murders. Even more time separated the next ones."

"Let me get this straight, Ms. James." Winston's tone was firm. "Are you saying that there could be another murder in a matter of days?"

"I think so. Nine days if we are being accurate, maybe sooner if there's something I'm missing. Who knows, maybe this was a one-off, but it seems more likely that if someone is copying the Ripper, there will be more, and soon."

Another murder... just a few days. Charlie began to get worried. "Arden, does your book talk about the Ripper?"

"The Shakespeare book? No, not really. It doesn't mention the Ripper at all. There is only one possible connection between my book and the Ripper that I can think of, but it doesn't make sense."

"Well," said Winston, "enlighten us anyway."

"My book does talk about a legendary group of people, the Templar Knights. They were a group of monks who had banded together in the 1100s to guard the Temple of Solomon and the city of Jerusalem in the name of Christ. This was during the Crusades. The organization grew and was eventually eradicated. However, it is thought that they went underground and eventually became what we know as the Freemasons. It is also thought that they took many incarnations and other names or forms during the years that separated 1307 when they were condemned, and 1717 when the first Masonic lodges went public. There are many interesting connections between Shakespeare and the Knights. I explore it in my book mostly because I hypothesize that Shakespeare was a Mason, or a form of Templar or early Mason known as a Rosicrucian. I look at different language and symbols in his texts which prove a link to the brotherhood.

"I look at everything from some possible general connections including the dedication in the first folio, to the symbology in the texts. The dedication states, 'To the most Noble and Incomparable pair of Brethren, ...the Earl of Pembroke, and the Earl of Montgomery.' Also, the reference in the dedication refers to Shakespeare as a worthy, 'friend and fellow' and that 'the most, though meanest of things are made precious when they are dedicated to the Temple.' Those references are vague, yet the brotherhood would have provided the source for the 'Temple' and the 'fellows'. I also talk about the headpieces which are Masonic squares, and—"

"Masonic squares? What are those?" Charlie was more confused now than ever.

"It is a shape created in perfect symmetry—the square and the compass. Look."

She made a star like shape with her hands.

Winston was getting visibly annoyed. "Arden," he said, "I have spent my life studying Shakespeare, and I truly do not see any connection to the Masons, and therefore, Jack the Ripper, in what you just said."

Arden took a deep breath. "As I said, the Templar Knights began as a group of monks which, during the Crusades, functioned to defend the Temple of Solomon. That's the most basic explanation. They somehow became quite wealthy and extremely powerful. In the early 1300's, however, King Philip of France became jealous of the Knights' power. There had not been any Crusades in a while, and he felt they had lost their purpose. The Pope at the time, Pope Clement, was a pawn of the King, who convinced him that the order had to be eradicated. On Friday, October 13, 1307, the Pope betrayed the Knights, and along with King Philip of France, sent out secret orders which caused the torture, arrest, and death of nearly all the Templar Knights in France. The Papal Edict condemned the entire order as traitors and heretics. It called for the capture of all the Knights, not just the ones in France.

"However, the political situation in Britain was quite different from that in France. The English were at war with Scotland. This order of Knights were warriors. The English and the Scottish needed them to help fight the war. The King of England, Edward II, ignored the Papal Bull for as long as he could. Unfortunately, Edward II was weak, and eventually allowed inquisitors into his country to seek out the Templars. By then, though, almost three full months had elapsed, and the British Knights for the most part had gone underground. Many went to Scotland, where the Papal Bull had not been issued. Most are just unaccounted for. The idea that they continued the order is backed up by various events in history, which took place after 1307. For example, later in the 1300s, you have the extremely well-organized Peasants' Revolt, which proved that somehow communication was traveling throughout the country with remarkable speed. Only a well-organized society would have been able to maintain that type of communication; one that allowed parts of the north and south of England to revolt simultaneously. The Templars were famous for their ability to transfer information. They are even credited with establishing the first organized banking system, which allowed Europeans in the Holy Land to access their fortunes at home."

"Peasants' Revolt?" Winston asked.

"Off the topic, I know, but there is a whole book about how the Peasants' Revolt proved the Knights had gone underground and orchestrated the Revolt. It is only relevant to Shakespeare in that he wrote a play about Richard II, who was king at that time."

"Richard II was only 14 at the time of the Peasants' Revolt." Winston seemed to understand where this was going.

"Yes," said Arden, "Richard II is portrayed as weak and despicable in Shakespeare's rendition."

"It is Shakespeare's version that most people think of as an accurate depiction of history."

"Yes, that's right. The Knights were supposedly eradicated, but since the British and Scottish Knights were never actually captured, the society continued. It established methods of communication, and organized different events, such as the Revolt, using various facades. Then, four hundred years after the Peasants' Revolt, only one hundred years after the death of William Shakespeare, a secret society unveiled its existence in London. The Grand Lodge of England came out of the closet, so to speak, in 1717. The group called themselves the Freemasons. But one thing I discuss in my book is one of the ways that they found to communicate during that undercover time was via travelling players and messages that were woven into plays."

"And Jack the Ripper?" asked Charlie.

"One of the most popular Ripper theories has the murders being orchestrated and carried out by a secret society known as the Freemasons."

## Chapter 12

**"Time shall unfold what plighted cunning hides:**

**Who cover faults, at last shame them derides." – *King Lear***

Alec raced along the riverbank. He had been thrown by the visitors, but not set off course. He had a job to do. He clutched the book close to him. The meeting would begin in a few minutes. He needed to speak to Peter and knew that once the meeting began, it could be hours before he would have a chance. The other book had been easy. No one had questioned him, and he knew that it would take ages before Winston noticed it was gone. He had been asked to get it and bring it to the lodge. His Benefactor had been perfectly right all along. It was all because of those damned symbols. Only certain levels of his brotherhood, only certain Masons were allowed to know the rituals, and here was some American girl spewing about Shakespeare, and Prospero, and the re-enactment ceremonies. Those were private. It was unbelievable to him that some American, someone outside of the inner circle, would know about such sacred experiences.

He had been beside himself when he found out. Alec was nothing if not loyal. Especially to his Benefactor. The Masons had been such an important part of his life. He owed everything to the Benefactor, and he didn't even know his true identity. He was not worthy of that, yet. There was no way he would let this book be sold at the Globe Theatre. It was treasonous. No one knew, of course. Well, that wasn't completely true. He hadn't been able to bring himself to tell anyone at the lodge at first. However, the feelings of guilt and betrayal had eaten away at him. In time, he confessed all to his Benefactor. Then he had told Peter. He had said too much to Peter, he knew, but Peter was a brother and a friend, so when Alec found himself telling all about the new book, he felt it was for the good of the whole. It wasn't anti-Mason. There were ample examples of such. Conspiracy theories galore. They included everything from who killed JFK to the "true" identity of the Bard himself. Alec hated those theories. Besides, everyone knew they weren't true. But if Shakespeare was a brother, that should remain private. Someone must know the truth, and there was a reason it wasn't public knowledge. It should stay that way. His mind raced as he ran towards the lodge. He couldn't be late to this meeting.

## Chapter 13

**"There is nothing either good or bad, but thinking makes it so." - *Hamlet***

"Wait a sec." Charlie was still taking in all he had just been told. "The Freemasons? Is that what *The Da Vinci Code* is about? I never got a chance to read it, but I thought I heard something about that. Or, wait, are they the people in *Bye Bye Birdie* with the funny hats?"

Arden laughed. "In *Bye Bye Birdie,* it is a branch that has Masonic origin, but no. They are not the Freemasons. They are called Shriners. I don't know too much about them, to be honest. Yes, *The Da Vinci Code* does talk about the Freemasons, so you heard correctly. See, there are many American branches of the Masons; there are branches all over the world. Historically, many prominent people have been Masons, including most of American's founding fathers. We—that is, America—are descended from Britain, after all, and as I said, the first recorded public outing of the Masons was in London in 1717. Many lodges were upset about the Grand Lodge of England going public, but by that time, it was safe. There is a great deal of Masonic lore that has to do with the principles of geometry and science. This is largely because Masons originally were builders who needed measuring tools to ply their trade such as the square and the compass which became symbols of Freemasonry. By 1717, we had entered the Age of Reason. The monarchy was losing its power, and the strong emergence of Protestantism had separated the Pope from the British Isles."

"Okay, no red hats, but what exactly does it have to do with Shakespeare?"

Winston responded first. "Your book alleges that Shakespeare was a Mason."

"Exactly.  Look, as I spoke about in my book, travelling players were one of the best sources of passing messages around the brotherhood as they could recite something quite innocent sounding to some, but which contained important information that others were waiting to hear. There are many places in the texts where there are references that clearly link Shakespeare to freemasonry. I mean, think about the plays he wrote. In a time where religion was so dominating, and satire hadn't been firmly established as a genre, you have these plays which—"

"Aren't really religious," Winston interjected with an air of boredom. "Meaning, there are many religious characters and references, but most of them are propaganda."

"Yes, exactly. Winston, you know how Christian symbols basically merge Roman or Pagan symbols and early Christian ideology?"

"Yes, I have heard such scholarly babble that many symbols were established as part of a political compromise by the Emperor Constantine. Of course, my dear. But I myself do not abide by such heretical theories. As you know, I am Catholic and feel strong in my faith. I am a man of learning to be sure, but when it comes to religious debate, I feel scholars should leave such things to the church. Faith is stronger than these scholars, or whoever they are, who have driven our Lord through the mud."

Arden was not surprised by Winston's reaction. She frequently argued with him about Shakespeare and religion. She never could understand his point of view. He was a scholar, wasn't he? She cleared her throat.

"Yes, well, Charlie, to let you know what that 'scholarly babble' as Winston says is, things such as the sun-god's crown became an angel's halo and, well, the whole holiday of Easter for that matter, the egg as a symbol of rebirth."

"That's pretty cool actually. I didn't know that."

"Yep. And then there is the whole Mary Magdalene theory."

"Hey, wasn't she the prostitute?" Charlie asked eagerly. Arden gave him a look. "What are you looking at me that way for? Give me a break here," he said, "I'm Jewish."

"So am I," laughed Arden. "I look at the symbols and the imagery, not at the religion. There are enduring legends that Jesus was married to Mary Magdalene. According to legend, she has been labeled as a prostitute in order to assure the deification of Jesus."

"And that is relevant because?" Winston was getting visibly uncomfortable.

"According to the same legend, the Knights were an armed branch of a society called the Priory of Sion. Their job to protect the Temple was really a cover up for protecting something much more valuable. It was something called the Holy Grail."

"*Indiana Jones and the Last Crusade*!" cried out Charlie. "Wait a second. That was a cup. The doctor guy drank from it, and he got all old and died."

Winston, interjected, “I don’t think that Indiana Jones is quite where we are going, and I certainly don’t appreciate important events such as the Crusades being scandalized by popular culture. This is really not what we are up against here.”

“I know, Winston, but he has a point of reference, and that’s what is important.”

Winston looked incredibly uncomfortable. He shifted in his seat, consumed in thought. After a moment, he came to life.

“Arden, I think we need to go to the site of the second Ripper murder,” said Winston, changing the subject.

“Now? Why? What good can it do?” Arden was confused.

“This is beginning to make sense to me and not in the way I would like it to. Oh, blast, it’s starting to rain. Come on, then. We can get taxis from the other side of the buildings, away from the bridge.”

With that, he got up and began walking away from the others.

Arden and Charlie exchanged looks but followed anyway. It was past lunchtime and after a few minutes, Charlie’s mind drifted towards the idea of eating. He was starving. And wet. He huddled next to Arden who had opened her umbrella.

“Hey, is there a McDonalds around anywhere?” No one paid attention to Charlie’s stomach.

“Winston, I don’t know that we need to head over there. I mean, even if there is going to be another murder, there were nine days which separated the murders. There are other things we should be doing, like concentrating on where Alec might have taken my book."

"I know where Alec took your book."

Arden stopped in her tracks, almost knocking Charlie over in the process. "What do you mean?"

Winston sighed, "Alec is a Mason." With that, he hailed a cab and the three of them rode in silence to Hanbury Street.

## Chapter 14

**"Mercy but murders, pardoning those that kill." - *Romeo and Juliet***

The scene at what was historically number 29 Hanbury Street was one of complete confusion. The rain had fortunately subsided to only a slight drizzle. The police had cornered off a large section of the road and the entirety of the block. However, despite their efforts, a massive crowd had gathered. Charlie grabbed hold of Arden's hand so he didn't lose her in the hysteria. They pushed their way ahead of Winston through to the front of the masses. There, to Charlie's surprise, was a tall and broad police detective speaking intently with Mr. Hendry.

"Richard? What are you doing here?" Arden was even more surprised than Charlie to see her supervisor. He was scheduled to be in meetings all day. She knew this because he had pointedly declined all interaction with everyone involved in the program.

"Arden. There you are. I have been calling your mobile for nearly an hour. Where have you been?"

"You've been calling me? I—oh. I turned it off for the meeting this morning and I guess I forgot to turn it back on."

Charlie looked behind him and saw Winston pushing his way through the crowd. He was still at a distance, so Charlie focused on the detective. Why, he thought, do all British people look at me as if I'm an insect that needs to be squashed?

The detective turned his attention away from Charlie and back to Arden. “Good afternoon, Dr. James. We seem to be meeting far too often. Who is your protégée, may I ask?”

“Charlie Leder, this is Detective Andrews.”

“Nice to meet you.” These niceties seemed ridiculous in the context of the massive swelling crowd around them. Winston seemed to be crowd-surfing now; Charlie didn’t see either of the old man’s legs touching the ground as he moved closer. Propelled by sheer will, Winston finally dropped down onto Charlie, causing the both of them to fall into the detective. Luckily, Detective Andrews managed to catch the old man and young student without so much as a whimper.

“Do we know this person?” The detective stood Winston up on his feet and dusted him off.

“Er, yes, actually. This is Winston Patrick, head of Globe Education and one of my mentors. He was helping me locate the remaining copies of my manuscript.”

“Well, Dr. James, search no further. If you will all follow me...” The awkward group stumbled into the street behind the police barricade. When they reached an area just past the street corner, the detective stopped short.

“Dr. James, do you know what you are about to look at?”

She nodded, walked a few paces up the street, and without missing a beat turned to look towards her left. There, before her, was the distinctive shape of a covered body. The others followed. Charlie, who had never seen a dead body before, was the first to speak.

"Can I see her? It's a girl, a substitute for a prostitute, right?"

"Someone's been paying attention to today's lessons," mumbled Winston. Detective Andrews did not appreciate Winston's dry humor. However, the disapproving look did not stop the detective from lifting the sheet, revealing the mutilated corpse.

"I think I'm going to be sick," Charlie whimpered as he turned away. He felt light-headed and dove for the nearby staircase to sit and steady himself.

Arden expected to feel just as sick as Charlie, but having looked at Ripper pictures so many times, she found herself only able to stare in saddened amazement. Everything, except the clothing the woman wore, was exactly as it had been over a century ago. This victim was lying next to the gate, flat on her back, with her throat cut. A flap of skin and her intestines were placed over her right shoulder. Above her left shoulder lay more skin and body parts. Her dress was saturated in blood.

Arden peered around. There were two rings placed near the body which indicated that the murder had to have an in-depth knowledge of different news stories which reported different items found at the murder scenes. Annie Chapman allegedly had two brass rings placed at her feet, but this detail was not common knowledge as it didn't appear in print until the early 20th century. The rings were not mentioned in the original inquest. Officially, at the scene of the original crime there had been an envelope. It was found near the body and contained two pills with no further description and although there was a mention of some 'odds and ends', there was no mention of rings until a book by Leonard Matters in 1928 who apparently got his information from a senior police officer. This was one of the many inconsistencies between the police case files, the newspaper reports, later written accounts of the murders and eyewitness testimony. For the rings to be there, the murderer had clearly studied more than the official Jack the Ripper casebook or had decided on a theory of his own. Arden's eyes canvassed the area, eventually resting on the spot where the envelope should have been. Instead of an envelope, she saw the manuscript. Her manuscript. But it wasn't the one from the Globe bookstore. That one had been bound in a beautiful brown leather cover. This one had black binding.

"Curious," she said without realizing she was speaking out loud.

"Quite, but is it yours?" The detective's words shook her out of her trance.

"Yes, but it isn't the one that went missing today. Whoever it was must have made a copy of the one from Winston's office."

"I'm sorry, Dr. James, missing today?"

"I went to the Globe to see if Winston still had the copy I had given to him. He didn't. While we were there, his assistant, Alec, took a copy that was on display at the bookstore. That one had a brown cover, though. This cover is black."

"Uh huh."

"And it's where the envelope should be."

"Envelope?"

"Placed near the body, Annie Chapman's body; there was an envelope with two pills in it. She had taken it from someone in her lodging. There have been all kinds of legends of different things placed near the body. See the rings? That's based on stories. However, in the original files, well, there is only a mention of the envelope. They had even investigated it. Annie Chapman had received it from someone in the house where she was lodging. There were drops of blood, which the reports say were as big as 'a sixpence.' Since then many rumors have flown about coins being left at the scene. There are legends of two farthings placed face up at the scene based on newspaper articles. I don't see them, but I see our man has done his homework and made specific choices. He has decided that the rings are real, but the coins are not. He would only know that if he was familiar with the original case files."

"And how would that happen? How would just anyone get a hold of the original files?" bristled the detective. Arden could see that he was assuming she was about to allege police impropriety. She had to dissipate any antagonism.

"Easily. Book, internet, anywhere. They were released to the public a few years ago."

Nearly placated, the detective continued, "And the rings and coins?"

"Different Ripper books, newspapers, many types of places have various records of things that may or may not have been at the scene."

Andrews thought for a minute before responding.

"What time was the book taken from the Globe gift shop?"

"Not long ago, maybe an hour?"

"And this woman was found dead approximately an hour ago."

"When was she killed?" Charlie asked.

"Our medical examiner has yet to determine that information, but we estimate just over an hour, and that she was killed elsewhere and brought here. There are far too many people who pass here to assume otherwise."

"Alec is a sketchy person, but he can't be in two places at the same time," Charlie pointed out.

"Thank you for pointing that out, lad, but I believe that is for me to decide. Right now, I request that you all come with me. We will reconvene back at my office to discuss this further. Mr. Hendry, I know you have obligations that you must attend to, so you may be dismissed. Would the rest of you please follow me? Dr. Patrick, would you please ring your assistant and tell him to join us? I would very much like to meet him."

With that, the haphazard group made their way back through the crowd. Hendry seemed extremely reluctant to leave, but a stern look from Detective Andrews told him there was no negotiating. Charlie longingly smelled the aroma of Indian food from a nearby restaurant.

## Chapter 15

**"I am Fortune's Fool." - *Romeo and Juliet***

It had only been a few moments after Peter had pretended to get a phone call that he had received a genuine call about the dead girl.

Another one, he thought.

He left his post and headed to the crime scene. When he arrived, he stood still, taking a moment to grieve for the girl as he always did. His mother's death had taught him that much. This one looked like her, too. Somehow, to Peter, all dead women looked like his mother.

"We have to hurry," came the voice.

"I know, Gov," Peter nodded without averting his gaze from the corpse. He took one more moment before turning to face his boss. "I'm off. I 'ave a meeting wiv someone who'd be terribly in'rested in this. I'll catch up wiv Arden again later."

"I will alert you when she is finished here."

"Finished? Is Arden coming 'ere?"

"Go to your meeting, lad. We will be in touch."

Peter watched the stern figure walk away. He turned one more time to the girl before walking back up the steps into the heart of London.

## Chapter 16

**"Oftentimes excusing of a fault, Doth make the fault the worse by the excuse" - *King John***

In the police car, Winston tried in vain to reach Alec.

"He's not picking up his mobile. He said he had a family emergency, but then again, something tells me that no family emergency would involve a three-hundred-page dissertation on Shakespeare."

Charlie stared out the window, willing it to open. He had already tried, but this was the back of a police car, meant to hold criminals. Nothing opened if the driver didn't open it. This particular police car was speeding at what felt like five hundred miles per hour on the wrong side of the road, and Charlie was afraid that his first car ride in London would result in him throwing up all over the other occupants of the vehicle. As if she could read his mind, Arden asked if they could open the back windows. The air was heaven to Charlie. After a few minutes, he was able to stop concentrating on holding back the nausea and able to look around.

The city was amazing. It was right out of a movie. The old buildings saturated the crazy inconsistent streets. Each building style of the past few hundred years seemed to overlap and blend into one another. He tried to follow the street names, but the names seemed to change every few blocks. *How does anyone find anything?* he thought. *Someone should really teach these people about grid systems.* He focused on the buildings. New buildings stood like glass straws next to the gothic cathedrals and stone houses. He wished he had paid more attention in art history to more accurately recognize the different styles and structures. He knew some of them were famous. Westminster Abbey? Which one was that? Big Ben? Was that the clock on the Houses of Parliament? Where was the Tower of London? Whatever they were, it didn't seem as though the streets were wide enough for the police car. This automobile sped through spaces that Charlie thought wouldn't fit a bike.

"Isn't it amazing?"

Arden's voice echoed his own thoughts.

"When London was bombed during the war, many buildings in the City of London were destroyed. The rebuilding is still ongoing, but like the Rose Theatre, it's happening on top of and next to the old city. Remember, The Rose was the one in the basement of that office building? See? Look over there. That hole in the ground was something, but now it's a scar—a reminder about the bombing. There are many buildings that are part of a national effort to maintain history. The City doesn't forget. It's pulsing with ghosts from ages past. Each building tells a story. Each person knows the stories. The City wants people to remember its past. It's not like in America. There, everything is constantly changing. Something gets torn down and a week later, you've forgotten the original building existed. Here, people want to remember, and everyone has a long memory."

"The City is beautiful. It looks like a string of sets from old movies," Charlie replied.

She looked at him softly and smiled. "If we have time before you go, I'd like to take you up north to the lake district. England is even more beautiful once you get out of the cities."

Charlie turned all his attention to Arden. He smiled back at her. Sitting so close to her, he realized she smelled like roses. *She really is beautiful*, he thought.

"I'd like that. I bet you make a great tour guide. I wouldn't even know what I should be looking at."

"It can be a sensory overload. Don't worry. I'll make sure you don't get overwhelmed."

"I believe you."

He smiled, forgetting for a moment that he was driving to Scotland Yard in the backseat of a police car.

"Look out the window. You don't want to miss anything," Arden said.

He turned back to the window and let his mind jump back to Cassie. She had hurt him deeply. He should have seen it coming. There were so many signs, but he was the quintessential romantic. He had fallen hard for Cassie and for a long time, she was the center of his world. All the obtuse excuses and nonsensical reasoning were brushed off as just being part of her and the relationship until the truth was right there in front of him. It had only been a few weeks, but still he was lonely. That was partly why it had been so hard to care about anything, especially this program. He had wanted to try to win her back, but she made it clear that was not something she was interested in. Flying off to a different country didn't leave the hurt behind, but somewhere inside he hoped it might make it more bearable.

The car finally stopped, and Charlie, Arden, and Winston unloaded themselves from the backseat. They were escorted up three flights of stairs to a corner office. It was smaller than Winston's yet had about twice as many things crammed into it. There were no figurines, though, or interesting posters. Instead of whisky, it smelled like old paper. There were photographs everywhere, and files. Lots and lots of files.

"Oh, my God!" Arden exclaimed, looking at a large, antiquated file box.

"My dear, is there a problem?" Winston and Charlie rushed over to the box.

"The original files. All the existing original Ripper files!"

"Yes, indeed they are, Dr. James."

"Where... how..."

"I am in charge of an investigation which seems to copycat the Ripper murders. I was given them to research. Something which I have yet to do in full."

"I've never seen the actual files. Not the physical documents themselves."

"Then may I ask, Dr. James," Detective Andrews' voice filled the room, "how does a Shakespearean scholar know so much about Jack the Ripper? Please, all of you, have a seat. And actually, before you answer that question, Dr. Patrick, I would ask you to wait outside. I would like to speak to these two charming Americans alone."

Winston opened his mouth to object, but suddenly seemed to change his mind and proceeded to the outside waiting room. Charlie and Arden sat. Andrews closed the door.

"You see, Dr. James, although I have not yet gone through all the files, it seems we have similar hobbies. What I have read fascinates me, and I fancy myself a budding Ripperologist. Now, what about you?"

"I have been interested in the Ripper for a long time. It is a hobby, really. If I'm interested in something, I like to read everything I can about it. I read one book and was hooked. It started when I began looking into Shakespeare as a Mason and I decided to learn more about the case. In fact, one of the Ripper theories that I don't entirely agree with involves the Masons. I was looking deeper into that theory and came across more Temp... I mean symbols, which I recognized existed in Shakespeare. Things like leather aprons, Pythagoras, Worshipful Masters, the Squares and the Rule; all masonic symbols and language. By then I had decided to concentrate on symbolism in Shakespeare. Prior to that, I was planning on writing a dissertation on a different aspect of Shakespeare—dreams. I do use dreams in my thesis, but in a different way."

"Shakespeare led you to the Masons, which led you to the Ripper, which led you back to Shakespeare?"

"Sort of. I mean, I got involved in Ripperology, which is really a separate interest. I still think of them as separate. The only thing that connects Shakespeare and the Ripper is the one Mason theory, and Masonic symbols in the plays I've studied that I just told you about."

"You became interested in Jack the Ripper, and in the middle of your research, stopped to write a book about him?"

"Yep. Especially after I saw the movie, *From Hell*. I was hooked."

"But the Ripper is not connected to Shakespeare?"

"Well, more or less indirectly related."

"Your conclusive nature will no doubt make this even easier," Andrews replied sarcastically.

"It's just not that cut and dry, Detective," Arden said.

"What was the theory that led you along this brilliant pathway?"

Before she could answer, something clicked in Charlie's mind. "Wait, the Masons. I haven't seen *The Da Vinci Code*, but I have seen *From Hell*."

"You know," she said smiling, "we both watch too many movies."

Charlie smiled at Arden and then looked at the detective. "That's probably true, but I do know what *From Hell* is about."

"Really. Then enlighten me. I am sorry to say I have not seen this cinematic masterpiece."

Charlie ignored Andrews' sarcasm.

"Prince Eddy, or Albert. He had syphilis. He had married a prostitute in a Catholic ceremony, Anne something, and they had given birth to a legitimate baby. This group of guys—the Masons—they went after Anne, made her go crazy, locked her up, took the baby away, or the baby ended up with this other girl; anyway, the doctor who was in charge of getting rid of Anne's friends, he helped the detective, but it was really him the whole time. He killed all the girls. This other guy was in charge of driving his carriage, and he gave them grapes and some drug, which Johnny Depp's character could smell on their lips. It was something similar to opium, and these other guys, including the police commissioner helped cover it up. Then the detective figured out what was going on, and the doctor went crazy and was locked up."

"Well done, Charlie. You just summarized Stephen Knight's whole theory as told by Johnny Depp and the Hughes Brothers and a load of other creative types that like taking the most dramatic conspiracy theory and incorporating it into modern pop culture."

"Do you mind filling in the pieces here, Dr. James? I admire how eloquently our dear boy has presented the rudiments of the case, but in the absence of last names and proper nouns, I find myself still needing an explanation. I am also curious as to how the monarchy is suddenly involved." Detective Andrews looked inquisitively at Arden who glared back at him.

"I'm sorry his summary was not good enough for you, but you really don't need to be so rude."

Andrews' reaction did not change with her disapproval, so she gave up and shifted back to the matter at hand.

"Well, as you know from the files, all the women who were killed were prostitutes. Years ago, a man named Joseph Sickert presented this theory to Stephen Knight, a British journalist. Sickert claimed he was the son of the painter, Walter Sickert, and Alice Margaret, the supposed legitimate child of Anne Crook and the Prince. The theory about Anne and Albert is based on a number of speculations. What is generally accepted is that Albert, or Eddy, died of syphilis in 1892. Officially, of course, he died of influenza, but oral legend had strongly suggested otherwise. He was very likely a member of the Masons. Knight alleges that Eddy secretly apprenticed for Walter Sickert. That's where he met Anne and married her in a Catholic ceremony and had Alice, a legitimate child. This would have been devastating for the monarchy on many levels. According to Knight and Joseph Sickert, Mary Kelly was friends with Anne and attended the wedding. Neither allegedly knew he was the prince. Once this marriage and baby were discovered, Dr. William Gull was charged with the task of disposing of Mary Kelly and anyone else who knew about the marriage. This task was assigned with the blessing and on the orders of the Masons. At this point, Knight alleges, all hell broke loose. Anne was given a lobotomy and sent to a workhouse. Mary and the other witnesses were killed. A carriage driver and a third man, whom Joseph Sickert claimed was the police commissioner at the time, Robert Anderson, allegedly assisted Gull. The carriage driver was a lower-order Mason named John Netley. Knight, however, claims that the third man was Walter Sickert himself, blackmailed into helping by providing information and such.

"The Joseph Sickert story was condemned as a hoax by Sickert himself after Knight's book was released. A few years later, Sickert said he was lying about saying his story was a hoax and insisted it was true. He said he had lied because of Knight's assumption that his father, Walter Sickert, was involved."

"Do you agree with this theory?" Andrews was listening intently, taking notes as he went along.

"Not all of it. Actually, in my opinion, hardly any of this story is possible or probable. I'm sure Joseph Sickert knew something which he learned from his father. That man is a shady character and a player in more than just the one Ripper theory. However, Knight's theory is not plausible. For one, there is proof that Annie Crook did not spend the rest of her life in a workhouse, and William Gull was old and had at least one, if not two strokes by 1888. He could not physically have executed the murders the way they occurred. Stephen Knight was extremely anti-Mason and, as far as I can tell, invented or tweaked evidence to fit his cause. For example, he has coins laid out at Annie Chapman's feet in the shape of a Masonic square. I have read the files, and according to all the testimonies made at the inquest, there is no mention of any coins found at the crime scene. That is part of the legend, not necessarily the facts.

"He states that the intestines were placed on the same shoulder as is pantomimed in a Masonic ceremony. In the ceremony, it is the left shoulder. Now, in the case of Catherine Eddowes, I believe, the intestines were placed on both shoulders. Wouldn't a Mason have been consistent? There are too many loose ends. The police were sent letters at the time, which came from 'Jack the Ripper.' While most of them are considered fake, some are thought to be authentic. It has been allegedly proven by Patricia Cornwell that Walter Sickert possibly wrote some of these Ripper letters. There is no doubt in my mind that he was somehow involved, but if so, I still do not believe he was the only Ripper. The link with the Prince is possible, but I believe that whoever the ringleader was in the Ripper murders, he was either a Mason acting without the blessing—indeed with the disapproval—of the brotherhood, or not a Mason at all and trying to frame them in some way. I tend to think the former. I agree that there must have been about three or so people involved; but Gull didn't rip anyone open, and who knows about Netley. The brotherhood is a secret organization. Even though they are known publicly, they pride themselves on the fact that they function to help each other. That may be an argument for them protecting Prince Eddy, but I don't believe that they would have backed a succession of brutal murders."

"This is getting far too complicated." The Detective sat back in his chair and rubbed his head.

"Wait, Arden." Charlie had been paying close attention and began to put everything together. "What exactly does your book do?"

"It floats the hypothesis that Shakespeare was a member of a secret society which I suggest was probably an evolution of the Templars and most likely a type of Freemasonry, or at least that his plays contained messages in the symbolism that would be recognizable when performed to members of the brotherhood in a time when the brotherhood had limited ways of communicating. Then it talks about some of the different symbols that might have been recognized."

"So," continued Charlie, "The Stephen Knight conspiracy with Prince Eddy has Masons protecting the monarchy. Your book connects Shakespeare to the Masons. These murders—the one the other night and the one we just saw—what if there was something in your book that gives away something? Some secret, which links the Masons or even a Mason to the Ripper murders. Or even just a secret that we aren't supposed to know? Winston said that Alec was a Mason and he stole your book. What if this guy is just using these murders to get to you, or to stop you from talking about his brotherhood?"

Arden shook her head.

"It doesn't make sense. I don't mention the Ripper at all in my book. I don't know how I would have even if I wanted to. The Freemasons of Shakespeare's day were so different from both the original Knights and the modern day Masons. All I do is point out Templar or Masonic symbols along with many other types of symbols. Nothing Ripper-like."

"What do they do? These Masonic symbols?"

"All they do is prove Shakespeare was linked to the organization. A secret organization, which at the time was not publicly known."

"Wait, Detective Andrews?"

"Yes, Charlie? You have a question which I may be able to answer?"

"Who were the girls? These two girls. What were their names?"

"Ah, yes. I was wondering when that would come up. I suppose they were 'prostitutes' in a matter of speaking. They were both actresses. They were employed by the same acting company. They both, it is my understanding, have been in rehearsal for some time for two different plays."

"I thought you said they were from the same company?" Arden asked.

"The same overall company. This company seems to have two different groups of actors which perform different pieces on alternating nights."

"Oh, God." Arden sucked in her breath. She knew it before anyone said anything. "The Red Company and the White Company. From the Globe. What were the plays? What were the parts?"

"Our lovely lady from yesterday was a bit player. She was in *Romeo and Juliet*. She played a boy's part actually: Samson. The girl killed today had a slightly larger role, also a man's role. She is... was... in *Macbeth*. She played the Porter."

## Chapter 17

**"'Tis an ill cook that cannot lick his own fingers." - *Romeo and Juliet***

The Benefactor was pleased with his day. Things were going as planned. Alec was a bit rash, to be sure, but the fools from America were nowhere near the truth. Dr. James was smarter than he thought, but she was no match for him. They would be chasing the wrong lead.

He smiled to himself as he pondered. She would leave them alone soon enough. He closed his eyes and began to pray. He must thank the Lord for all his work. He must never turn away from the Creator. Wasn't it His doing? People should not violate the laws of heaven. They would be punished.

The Benefactor had been astonished at the amount of blasphemy floating about. He knew that there needed to be an end to it. The matter had troubled him for some time. He sighed as he thought of the years he spent praying for a manner in which to stop this slander from overshadowing the beauty that was the true way. He had shared his concerns with his Brother who agreed whole-heartedly that action must be taken. Then, he heard of the American girl and her symbols and theories. That was the final straw.

The plan had been right in front of him the whole time. Finally, the Lord granted him the power to see, and victory became attainable. It was a simple plan. One of which he was quite proud. Everything was coming together nicely, just as he knew it would. It would not be long now.

## Chapter 18

**"Murder's out of tune, And sweet revenge grows harsh." - *Othello***

Alec's meeting had not gone as he had planned. It had not gone at all, actually. Peter had not been there. Peter never missed a meeting. In addition, Alec's voice mail was filled with messages that Winston had left for him which were not exactly comforting. What could the old man want, anyway? Reluctantly, Alec called Winston back. The voice on the other end of the line seemed tired and distant.

"Alec, there you are. Where on earth are you?"

"I told you, sir, I had a family emergency."

"Well, hang your emergency. I need you to come to Scotland Yard at once. And bring the damned book. I don't know why you took it in the first place."

"I'm sorry, sir, that is not possible."

"Which part? You still have the book, don't you?"

"I have orders, sir. I have the book, which, as it happens is a matter of great importance. I must keep my word. I apologize, sir, but I cannot bring you the book."

"There's been a murder, damn it. I need you to—"

Alec hung up the phone. Another murder. He heard about the first one at the meeting. It had surprised him, but he'd been instructed not to discuss it any further. It was none of their business. The Grandmaster had been strict. Alec wondered where Peter had taken the first book. Alec had removed it from Winston's office at Peter's request but then never got it back. Now, this second book had a specific destination. Winston would be unhappy, but Winston was always unhappy. Come to think of it, why was the book important to anyone at Scotland Yard? He would wait for the Benefactor. The Benefactor would know what Alec needed to do.

**Chapter 19**

**"Truth is truth To th'end of reck'ning." - *Measure for Measure***

Arden stood up and walked towards the file box. She knew there was a sinister significance to the fact that Globe actresses had been killed. It wasn't just the actresses; it was the roles they played.

"Are you okay, Arden?" Charlie asked.

"Is there something I can help you find, Ms. James?" asked the Detective.

"In my book, there are a few... well, Samson, the name... It stands for... The early Freemasons were known as Sam's sons. Solomon's sons from the Temple of Solomon. The Temple allegory is more prevalent in other Shakespeare plays such as *Love's Labour's Lost* and especially in *The Tempest,* but in the absence of these works... If you had to choose two characters in either *Romeo and Juliet* or *Macbeth* ... I'm getting ahead of myself."

Arden sighed as she ran her hands gently over the aged documents. She was beginning to feel like a broken record. She turned back to Andrews.

"One of the strongest connections between Templars and Freemasons is the role of the Tyler, or the Porter. He stands guard of the door to the meeting. It takes a special knock to let in those who will be initiated to a higher degree, a special knock for each degree, et cetera. Also, if there was a threat to the meeting, the Porter guards against it. In an era where the very existence of the society could mean death, the Porter was vital to the protection of the organization. This is also a society that has accepted and encouraged an early type of religious freedom. If you look at the Porter in *Macbeth*, he rambles about the knocking and about the devil. Many of the Porter's references in *Macbeth* are Masonic. Therefore, the two people who have been killed are both people who play parts that I talk about in my book. They are both links between Shakespeare and the Masons."

Andrews thought for a few minutes. "Well, now. I think we have ourselves a treasure hunt."

"Pardon?"

"You won't be aware of this, Dr. James, I've been getting strange messages almost daily in the mail. They seem to be quotes. I have about 15 of them, to date. Some I know as quotes, others I don't."

"You've received quotes?"

"Threats are more accurate. We have been investigating, but we have no idea what they mean."

Arden nodded. "They were warnings."

Andrews posture stiffened in his chair, suddenly becoming even more serious. "What I do know is that something is happening. I worry there will be three other murders. At least, there will be if this is not solved. Thank you for telling me about the crimes that are being staged. I accept that you have a greater background in Shakespeare to see these connections, but I must warn you that I do know of the Masons, and there are powerful people in that brotherhood. People within who would strongly object to anything which publicly involves their organization. This is a delicate matter." Almost inaudibly, Andrews continued, "The publicity which would come from these investigations would bring about mass hysteria, within these walls alone. If they knew that two Americans were remotely connected with such an investigation and were implicating the Masons, again... I am aware that you are capable of putting the pieces of this puzzle together. However, you two are Americans, and this boy... well, you understand, Dr. James, you have the problem of having your work now becoming part of this investigation and have the even greater misfortune of possessing a great deal of knowledge on this subject. However, I hope you understand; I need you to say nothing to anyone outside this room."

"But—" Arden began.

"I'm sure you understand," Andrews interrupted, still sotto voce, "you and this boy are on your own. If anyone asks me about you, I must be able to formally deny any and all knowledge of your existence."

Arden and Charlie looked at each other and nodded. Arden most definitely did not understand and could not fathom any "mass hysteria" from her being American or Charlie being a student.

Andrews looked intently at Arden.

"You will leave this investigation alone. I must insist that although you must keep me informed of your whereabouts, you also must separate yourself from any future involvement unless I notify you that I might require your assistance."

"But—" Arden began.

"I'm sure you understand," Andrews interrupted, "you and this boy are on your own.

Arden, confused, tried one more time to understand.

"Detective, I...?"

"That will be all, Dr. James," Andrews said aloud then added in hushed tones, "Oh, and Dr. James, contact me immediately if you should accidentally, while minding your own business, find anything that is remotely of interest."

Andrews stood up and opened the door. "Good day to you both" he said for all to hear.

Arden and Charlie understood that this meeting was officially over.

Andrews looked into the waiting room and glanced over at Winston who was madly redialing a number on his cell phone. "Dr. Winston," summoned Andrews, "it is your turn. Your colleagues will not wait for you. They have been dismissed and discharged from this building."

Arden and Charlie didn't even look in Winston's direction as they left. Exiting the building, Charlie turned to Arden. "So, he wants us to be a part of this without actually acknowledging that we are?"

"It certainly does seem that way," Arden agreed. "I guess he knows that he needs information from me but doesn't want to admit it. I mean, aside from everything else, how many times over the course of the past five minutes did he point out that we were American?"

"You have a point there," Charlie laughed. "So, Miss American James, what exactly should we do now?"

"It's Dr. American James to you," she snickered back. "And I think we should start at the beginning. Let's get out of here and find somewhere we can talk."

"Your place?"

"No, I don't know. I mean, what if the person who stole my book has my place bugged or something?"

"Paranoid much?"

"Not paranoid. Concerned."

Charlie thought for a moment before speaking.

"Food?" he asked hopefully.

That got a laugh.

"Okay, food. We'll find a place to eat and re-evaluate from there." Arden looked around as they began to walk away from New Scotland Yard. The streets were crowded, but she knew something was wrong. She paused and looked behind her.

"What's the matter?" Charlie asked.

"I don't know. I thought I saw something. It's nothing, I guess. I'm just imagining things. Food sounds like a good idea. Maybe I'm just hungry, too. I think."

As they walked off into the cool but dry London air, Peter followed about ten feet behind. Panting from having just returned from his meeting, Peter realized he had just stepped in a pile of dog shit.

"Blast," he muttered. He tried to wipe it off.

"Blast again. They walk too bloody fast." He stopped wiping his shoe and hurried after the two Americans.

## Chapter 20

**"Watch out he's winding the watch of his wit, by and by it will strike." - *The Tempest***

Edward Filbin, the Grandmaster in the third degree of Lodge Number 21, was having a really bad day. The meeting had gone well enough, but there were a few members missing who had been key parts in the ceremony. Those parts had to be recast at the last moment, and Edward had not been pleased. In addition, his niece, who had recently been cast in the Red Company of the Globe Theatre, was found brutally murdered the day before. His family was still reeling from the discovery, but what was most strange was the way it had occurred. There were brooding similarities to this killing that he could not easily overlook. He was ready to head home for a nice cup of tea before work (which would be hell also) when he was told that Alec, one of the stranger members of the Order, was lingering outside as if he was waiting to speak with him. He had taken as much time as possible getting ready but could not find any other way of procrastinating. Edward sighed.

"Let him in."

Alec rushed in, speaking immediately. "I'm sorry to keep you like this, but things have happened of the most grave nature. I don't know if you are aware, sir, but I am Assistant Education Director of the Globe Theatre. Recently, a young woman wrote a manuscript linking Shakespeare to the Order. Well, naturally, I was appalled, but I did not know what course of action to take. I had borrowed a copy of the manuscript and showed it to Brother Peter. He took it from me and assured me there would be no further involvement on my part. Unfortunately, the girl came looking for it, and—"

Edward interrupted before Alec could keep going. "I don't suppose that this has anything to do with the young lady that was found murdered yesterday evening?"

Alec stopped in his tracks.

"I'm not sure if you are aware, Brother," Edward began, "the lady was my niece. I fully intend to see that her killer is reprimanded in the most severe meaning of the word possible. I have one question. Was the title of this masterly work *Shakespeare and Symbolism*?"

"Yes sir, it was. How did you..." Alec's voice trailed off.

"There was a book of that name found at the murder scene. A murder scene, which closely resembled a different murder scene. One from long ago."

"Yes, sir. I know."

"Then you know how important it is to be cautious. Tell me about the author."

"She is a young teacher. She is here with a friend. They came looking for copies of the book. The one I had given Peter is gone. This one is from the display at the Globe bookstore."

"Thank you, Alec. You may go."

"But sir, I—"

"You will leave the book with me and you will go. You will discuss this with no one. I have work to do."

Alec, having no other choice, began to leave the room. "Sir, I'm afraid what you ask is impossible. I came to you for a reason, but..."

Edward grabbed the book from Alec.

"Thank you. I will return this to where it belongs."

Alec stood still for a moment. He was a coward, however, and as tall as Alec was, Edward was a much bigger man. All Alec could muster, "You will be hearing from me again," and with that, Alec left.

Edward shook his head. Alec was a strange one. At that, Edward turned around, sat at his desk, and picked up the phone.

"Scotland Yard, please... Detective, he just left. Yes, I have the book."

## Chapter 21

**"The hand that hath made you fair hath made you good." - *Measure for Measure***

Food. Deep-fried fish with some floppy, giant fries (which the waiter had called chips) next to it, smelling of grease, but at least it was food. Once his hunger was abated, Charlie turned his mind to the situation at hand. Arden slowly munched on a sandwich. "Why," asked Charlie, "do you think he's killing actors?"

"It's not the actors so much as the characters. I suppose there are only two plays he has to choose from... If they were doing *The Tempest*, it would be a different story."

"Why's that?"

"*The Tempest* is thought to be Shakespeare's most Masonic play. It's thought that he wrote it in honor of a man named John Dee, who was Queen Elizabeth's chief astrologer. He belonged to a school of thought known as Rosicrucian. We talked about the Holy Grail before. The Rosicrucians believed that Mary Magdalene was without a doubt the wife of Jesus. She was in fact the living Holy Grail. From her came Jesus' child, which began a line of princes. The Rosicrucians exposed the idea that the documents which proved this were protected by a powerful brotherhood."

"The Masons?"

"The Priory of Sion, a society that originally established the Templars as a fighting arm for protection and to guard Jesus' homeland. In fact, Robert Fludd, who was the head of the Priory of Sion during Shakespeare's time, was an ardent Rosicrucian. So was Francis Bacon, whom many argue wrote Shakespeare's plays. It is thought by some that the Rosicrucians were a possible incarnation of the Templar Knights who continued their traditions, eventually outing themselves as Masons."

"Wouldn't something like Jesus having a baby completely destroy Christianity as we know it?"

"Well, not really. I mean, these ideas have been around for a long time. I suppose if anyone were to find documented proof of the Christ bloodline, it would cause a huge stir. Well, let me rephrase that. People have found evidence of a Christ bloodline, but there are some gaps, and nothing has been proved incontrovertibly. Anyway, it is irrelevant whether the theory is true. I've read about it, and it seems quite plausible. I don't think it would destroy anything, though. Religion is strong, but it is also adaptable. Even Catholicism. There have been documents already found which have caused massive controversy about the nature of Christ's humanism. That doesn't stop Catholics from going to church."

"So why is this important?" Charlie was getting impatient now. This seemed to be going nowhere. Just a bunch of random information, which didn't seem to connect, and didn't seem to relate to some guy in the 1800's killing people.

"It is easy for an institution like Catholicism, or any sect of Christianity, or Judaism... any religion, to pick up and move on. As I said, religion is adaptable. Adam and Eve got a beating when Darwin came up with the theory of evolution. That didn't stop people from believing in God. Nor did it erase the creation myth from our vocabulary. I mean there are some crazy people who will *only* teach creationism and shun the scientific theories, but most people do not think the world was really created in seven days. You see?"

"I guess so, but can you make this relevant? Secret societies, the Masons, those Knights, the people with the long R name. How is it sacred then?"

"Okay, well think about fraternities."

"Fraternities?" Charlie felt like he had just entered a different conversation. "Where do we get fraternities? We were talking about God."

"I know, exactly. Tell me about the frats at your school."

"Okay," Charlie said slowly. He didn't see the connection, but he knew about frats. He was a member of one. "I hated pledging. It was complete hell. Once we get past that, though, it's just a place where we go, hang out, party, drink beer, and, well, what else can I tell you?"

"My sorority had a secret handshake."

"Well, yeah, there are secret things we do; we don't talk about them to non-brothers."

"Do you think the world would collapse if your frat stopped existing?"

"Not collapse, but it would be sad. I mean, I love that place. My brothers are awesome. We take care of each other."

"Is there an initiation ceremony?"

"Of course, but again—"

"You can't talk about that."

"Well—"

"And there are things brothers do... like cheat on a test or something, but since you're brothers, you don't talk about it."

"Yeah, but that's just brotherhood. You know. We protect each other."

"If one of your brothers was Jack the Ripper... what would you do?"

Charlie thought about this for a minute. He tried to picture some of his brothers as Jack the Ripper. All he could picture was his brother Jay passed out on the couch with a trashcan under his head and about five guys with markers writing on his arms. He laughed out loud thinking about it. That happened nearly every Saturday night.

"It would be funny?"

"No, no, I was thinking about something else. I really can't picture that."

"Well, basically, that's the type of thing we are talking about here. We are talking about a huge number of people protecting a secret. Not a secret of the Brotherhood, but a secret of one or two men. Men who did something evil in the name of the Brotherhood. With or without the blessing of the group, the inner circle would protect and possibly even pass judgment on their own. They would not involve outsiders in their rituals."

"Are you sure they are Masons? I mean, are you sure the Ripper was a Mason?"

"I wasn't before. I'm still not convinced that all the people involved in the Ripper killings were Masons. But after today, you'd be hard-pressed to convince me that at least one of the people involved in the murders wasn't high enough in the Brotherhood to possess a certain amount of knowledge. And high enough in the order that many decades of men have gone out on a limb to protect him."

"It sounds so dramatic. I mean, my brothers spend their time getting drunk and picking up girls... or trying to at least. Some aren't so successful."

"What about you?" Arden asked. Charlie wasn't expecting that.

"Okay, change of subject... I just got out of a long-term relationship; cheating. I should have seen it coming, but I loved her. I didn't want to see it. It just happened a few weeks before I came here. I'm not... well, I guess I'm over it. I don't know. Part of me wants her back. Is that crazy?"

"Crazy that you want to date someone who cheats on you? Yes. Without a doubt. Is that why you came here? To run away?"

"I think so. Well, I don't know. I received this scholarship and I guess I was running away, but I would have come anyway. I think I would have. I don't know. It's been a really confusing few weeks. And the last couple of hours haven't helped."

"This must have taken your mind off it at least. I mean, murders are a good distraction"

Charlie smiled. "Yes. I have definitely been distracted from my misery. Without passing out on any couches." *And by you*, Charlie thought, but didn't add out loud.

"See, I have been good for something."

"What about you?" Charlie asked. "I mean, you must have a boyfriend or something."

"No. I was dating someone, but we broke up a few weeks ago." Arden replied frankly. "I know I can come across as fiercely independent, but the truth is that one day, I do want to settle down and get married, but I just haven't met that right person and I've been so involved in my studies and career that I haven't really had a chance to look. To tell you the truth, I don't even know what I'm looking for."

"Other than Jack the Ripper?" Charlie asked jokingly.

"If we find this Ripper, I guarantee he is not going to be someone I settle down with." She laughed. "I thought the last guy might have been the right person. I really liked him."

"What happened?" Charlie asked.

"I don't know, to be honest. One minute everything was great, the next day, he was gone. I don't know what went wrong."

Charlie was quiet for a minute. "It's gets lonely, doesn't it?" he asked.

"All the time." Arden smiled wryly. "But I don't let it get to me. If it starts to, I go and sit by the Thames and think about all the good things I have. The feelings pass and I move on. What else can I do?"

"Is that what you were doing the other morning when I met you?"

She laughed. "I had forgotten about that. Yes, I suppose I was. I had woken up in the middle of the night and felt scared. I don't know. I looked over as if he, that last guy, was there, but he wasn't. My neighbors were having a party. I thought about going, but I wasn't in the mood for that, ya know? Sometimes I just need to be alone, so I don't feel lonely. Is that weird?"

Charlie thought for a moment. "No," he said smiling, "it actually makes perfect sense."

Silence filled the moment as the two of them looked at each other.

Arden was the first to speak. "I suppose we should get back to the girl who was killed; we have a job to do."

"Yes. So, umm," Charlie needed to focus back on the situation at hand. "What do we know so far?"

"We know that someone is killing Globe actors in the style of Jack the Ripper. He is picking people who play roles that exemplify various aspects of the Templar Knights and Freemasons. Roles which link the two together."

"Okay, well let's think about that guy, John Dee. He was a Mason?"

"I think so. He at least was part of a school of thought that stemmed from or led to the Masons."

"Is there anything else in either of the two plays—any characters I mean—that might be a link?"

"Well, let's think about this. Dee was an occultist. There are plenty of occult symbols in *Macbeth*. I mean, the witches are all about the occult."

"What about the other play, *Romeo and Juliet*?"

"Mercutio has the Queen Mab speech. But I know he's played by a guy. There's the Friar, he dabbles in herbology, and then there's the Apothecary, but they are all played by male actors in this new Globe production."

"So let's focus on *Macbeth*."

"First Samson, that was from *Romeo and Juliet*, but it could be a clue to point us in the right direction. Solomon's sons. Then the Porter; the person who opens the door."

"Then the witches?"

"Possible. I'm not sure where else he has to go. I mean there's Hecate, but that scene is usually cut, and I think it's cut from the Globe version, so then there would be no Hecate; she's queen of the witches."

"What about Lady Macbeth?"

"It's possible. She has a line in which she talks about being the serpent. That has been thought of as a Biblical reference. It's too small, though. I think we are on the right track with the witches. There are three of them, and three more Ripper killings."

"Are they in rehearsal?"

"Well, they have to recast the Porter role."

"So, maybe it's time to pay a visit to the director?"

"Charlie, I think you are absolutely right."

## Chapter 22

**"O, brave new world that has such people in't!" - *The Tempest***

Edward was waiting for them. He had to take his tea in a to-go container and rush over to rehearsal. His wife was furious with him for not going home to be with the family, but in addition to mourning the death of his niece, he had to recast the damned role. He had cast her as the Porter in a last minute rush. The man who was supposed to play the Porter had suddenly backed out. That was then. Now, things were different. He had lost a niece and a valuable actor. Now he was sitting in the rehearsal room, having calmed a cast of shaken actors, trying to decide who would take over the role.

The voice of his assistant drifted into his thoughts. "Sir, there are two young people here to see you. I wouldn't have interrupted you, but they assure me it is extremely important."

Miles, Edward's assistant, did not seem to feel the urgency that Arden and Charlie had impressed upon him, but as they would not go away, he had no choice but to interrupt rehearsal.

"Send them in." Edward figured they would arrive here sooner or later. Especially after his conversation with Andrews, he knew that Arden in particular would figure out the connection. He had looked over the text given to him by the unwilling Alec and realized that he needed to treat this with the utmost delicacy. She knew quite a bit, although she probably didn't know how much. He turned to his directing assistant and announced that he would work on the Porter problem later. If someone else in the cast felt like suddenly being double cast, of course, that would speed up the process.

"Mr. Filbin?" Arden and Charlie had appeared in the doorway.

"Yes, yes. Miles, take over rehearsal. Whoever you choose to read the part now will be fine. Just make sure it's a man. Come with me, you two."

He led them through the hallway and down the stairs to the Green Room. "We should be okay here. I don't think anyone will bother us."

"Do you know why we need to see you?" Arden asked.

"I would imagine it has to do with your book being left at a crime scene involving the demise of not only one of my stronger comic actors, but my niece."

"Oh, I'm so sorry for your loss. And you know—"

"That there has been a second murder? Yes, I do. What I don't know is what the hell is going on around here."

"She was your niece?" That had stopped Charlie in his tracks. He might not be a scholar, yet, but he had watched enough episodes of *Law and Order* to know that something was a bit too convenient about this.

"Yes. She was. And, what is not common knowledge, and what will not become so, is what I am about to tell you. I am also a member of an extremely protective brotherhood which I believe you, Dr. James, are all too familiar with."

"You're a Mason?"

"Yes. I am in fact a Master Mason. Of course, I can't discuss that with you. All I can say is more than just my career is affected by this."

"What about Alec? Winston's assistant?"

Edward laughed. "Alec is only an apprentice-level brother. He is not even aware that the head of our brotherhood is not myself. He knows me as the Grandmaster, which I am at the lodge level, but there are district levels. However, as apprentice, Alec has not earned the right to the knowledge of the higher ranks."

Arden nodded. "I understand."

"Good, because if you didn't, I could not explain it to you. Now, what I am going to ask is whether you have any idea who killed my niece."

"I'm afraid I really don't. All we have been able to do is figure out who might be next."

"Might be next?"

"Yes. The Ripper killed five people. So far, two people have died. That leaves three more possible victims."

"So, you want to know whom from my company might be next?"

Charlie's eyes wandered around the room. On one side of a small table there was a model of a building. It was unique yet strangely familiar. Charlie knew he had never seen it before, but he had pictured something like it when...

"No, actually, we don't," Charlie interrupted before Arden could speak. "Have you recast the role of the Porter?"

"Not yet. I believe that is what my assistant is doing as we speak," Edward said, eyeing Charlie with suspicion. Suddenly a voice squawked out of the walkie-talkie clipped to Edward's waist. "Edward, please come to the stage right away."

Edward rolled his eyes. "My assistant *should* be doing as we speak, I should say. Dr. James, if you would be so kind, please excuse me."

He turned and walked out of the room.

"Charlie, what are you doing? We know who the next victims will be. We need to make sure they are protected, watched or something."

"I know, I know, but there's something about this that doesn't fit. You know that building you were talking about before?"

"Building? What building?"

"That gatehouse thing."

"Yeah, the gatehouse, but what does that have to do with anything?"

"I'm not sure, but I think we should go there."

"Go where? It doesn't exist anymore."

"But something is there, right? And something might have replaced what was important about the old one."

"Blackfriars station is there. It's been extended over the river." Arden thought for a moment. "But actually, the gatehouse was further down. Closer to London Bridge and I can't remember exactly what building is on the exact spot now. But shouldn't we wait for—"

"No. I think we should leave. Right now."

Charlie and Arden had no sooner walked out of the office when they saw shadows of three men walking down the hallway towards them. Charlie frantically looked around. He spotted an emergency exit, grabbed Arden, and the two clambered down the exit stairway. They ran away from the warehouse just as voices yelled after them, "Stop them, they're getting away!" Charlie and Arden kept running until they were safely out of range and hidden. Luckily, the streets were so twisted that there were about three different roads leading out towards the Thames.

Arden led the way, and when she felt they were out of earshot, she said, "What just happened?"

"I don't know. Something was just wrong with the whole thing. I mean, not just an actor, but his niece? Why was she playing that role? And he knew way too much for a guy who should be directing a play. I mean, when I'm working, I don't pay attention to anything. There was just something wrong about the whole thing. Then I saw that he had a model of an old building that looked like what I would describe as a gatehouse on his table."

"I wonder what he wanted from us. And all that stuff about not being able to talk about anything? Something is weird about this whole thing. There is obviously something the Brotherhood doesn't know, but thinks it should know, and thinks that we know what it should know. Or maybe it knows, and thinks we know, but we don't and they don't believe us?"

"That sentence made no sense whatsoever."

Arden's cell phone rang. She hesitated and looked for a minute. "It's Winston," she said.

"Hello? Yes, we're fine. Just... getting something to eat. Charlie's awfully hungry. The Sussex? Yes, I know where that is. Okay, ummm... fifteen minutes? Okay, we'll be there."

"He wants to meet us?"

"Seems that way. We'll go to where the gatehouse was afterwards. It's not massively far from where we'll be, which, by the way, is one of my favorite parts of London. It's always mobbed, though, so keep your eyes open."

"I always do," Charlie said with a grin.

He started following Arden but tripped on the stone steps.

"That was smooth," he said.

"Absolutely," Arden snickered. "Be careful. These streets are old. Cobblestones and all. The rain makes them slippery." Arden paused then teased, "Maybe you should hold my hand."

"Well, maybe I should. You never know. This strange city might get the better of me if you can't keep me from killing myself in the street."

Arden laughed again and held out her hand. Charlie took it and they walked down the street. About ten feet behind them, a voice muffled a painful wince as the speaker slipped on the same step in a hurry to catch up.

## Chapter 23

**"Good wombs have borne bad sons." - *The Tempest***

Winston would have been pacing if he could have. His legs hurt and it had been a long day. Hendry... why the devil had he been there? What was Andrews about with all his random questions? Where the devil was Alec? And Peter, the actor who played Mercutio, had been missing for the last few days. Everything was beginning to move a bit too quickly. He downed his pint and waited anxiously for the two Americans to arrive. Suddenly a hand fell down hard on his shoulder.

"Peter, you devil. You scared the life out of me. Everyone's looking for you."

"I'm sorry, Paddy old boy." Peter had a way of making everything into a joke. And he especially liked how much Winston Patrick hated being called Paddy yet refused to do anything other than wince when Peter used the nickname. "Who's lookin' for me?"

"Your director, for a start. Do you know that you have an emergency rehearsal now? Your 'Samson' has been murdered."

"Murdered, really? Fancy that." Peter did not seem as surprised as Winston had anticipated. "And what are you doing here, then? Don't you have some fixin' up to do?"

"If you must know, I'm meeting some friends. Globe business."

"You're awfully far from the Globe, Paddy. There are 'alf a dozen great pubs all wifin a 'alf mile."

"Yes, well, a friend from America has a visitor with her. He wanted to see more of London. And this is the most exciting part of the city. What, may I ask, are you doing here?"

"Just 'anging out. Me mates work 'ere. What a better place to spend me afternoon."

"Winston, there you are." Arden's voice broke the tension. "And Peter." She paused in astonishment for a moment. "I didn't expect you to be here."

Peter knew this moment would come eventually. He had waited for it. He needed everything to go smoothly. Looking at her again face to face, however, was just much harder than he thought it would be. He took a deep breath. Focus, he said to himself. I'm Peter. I'm a player, I'm obnoxious, and I'm only around 'cause of my job. Remote. Sarcastic.

"I'm just full of surprises today, mate," he heard himself say. "I didn't know you were the friend Paddy was meetin'. And who's your lit'l boy toy then?"

"This is Charlie. He's visiting. From America."

"A little young for you, I reckon, Arden. Feelin' old, are you? That's the beauty of being a professor, I guess. To quote a famous movie, 'You get older; they stay the same age.' And this one's a ringer."

Charlie didn't like this guy. "I've seen *Dazed and Confused* also. Who are you trying to be? The creep who beats freshmen with a paddle? Or the girl who throws all kinds of crap on people?"

"He's got spunk, Arden. Gotta give that to ya. Well, I 'ave to be going now. Got some important business of me own t' take care of."

"And what would that be, Peter?" Arden snarled.

"Wouldn't you like to know, luv," he turned to Winston. "I'll be seein' you lot very soon, I'm sure. Ta ta, all."

They watched Peter as he pushed his way out of the crowded pub.

"Who was that asshole?" Charlie asked.

"That was Peter. He plays Mercutio in *Romeo and Juliet*." Arden's face was dark as she spoke.

Winston pulled himself together and proceeded with the business at hand. "Yes, well, I don't know what he was on about."

"What did you want, Winston?" Arden did not enjoy being made to look a fool. She hated Peter for breaking her heart. It had been so great at the beginning. He had been so sweet. Then, without warning, he had turned sour on her. What made matters worse was there had been no explanation. She had been finishing her dissertation. He had come by one day and asked to read it. She let him, and the next day, he was gone. That was it. Now, every time she saw him, he was either mean or ignored her. There was neither rhyme nor reason for any aspect of his behavior.

"That's an awfully ignorant question considering the circumstances, Arden. A woman is found with her intestines pulled out of her body and thrown over her left shoulder and all you can say is 'What do you want?'"

"They were over her right shoulder," Charlie corrected.

"Right shoulder, left shoulder, what does it matter? The point is, that detective actually thinks Alec has something to do with this, can you believe that? And why the devil can't I get a hold of him? The bloody wanker won't answer his bloody phone."

"What do you know about the Templar Knights, Winston?" Arden asked.

"What do I know about the... only what you told me before. Look, what I want to know is what the devil does my theatre have to do with this mess?"

"Winston, if you think about it and if you read my book, you would know that the Globe is the ultimate tribute to the Knights."

"I don't follow."

"Neither do I," piped in Charlie.

"'This Wooden O...'" began Arden.

"Yes, what does the quote from *Henry V* have to do with anything? Was Henry a Knight Templar?"

"The O shape. Round. It's the same shape as... The Knights were dedicated to protecting the temple of Solomon. Christianity, in its present form, is a mix of pagan and early Christian symbols. The shape is a tribute to the principles of Sacred Geometry."

"We've already covered that," Charlie interjected.

"Pagan churches, and indeed early temples were round. The Temple Church in London is recognized as a Templar design. The original Globe was built during Robert Fludd's tenure as head of the Priory of Sion. As were the Rose Theatre and The Theatre in what is now Shoreditch. All of them are wooden Os. If there was someone who was trying to make some type of statement about the Brotherhood, the Globe is a good place to start."

"The Temple Church is a sacred space. How dare you speak of it as pagan!" Winston fumed.

"The church isn't pagan; the shape is what's important. As a symbol. Anyway, it's not the Church that matters here. It's the Globe."

"But if all these symbols are Christian..." Charlie was still trying to put things together.

"What did I tell you before, Charlie? This has nothing to do with religion."

"Then what does it have to do with?" Winston was furious now.

Arden looked at him, but before she could answer, Charlie came alive.

"It has to do with someone who has strong feelings of either hate or love towards the Brotherhood," Charlie exclaimed. "If it's hate, he hates it so much, he wants to make sure it takes the blame for a crime that he's re-creating for the sole purpose of seeking revenge against the organization. If it's that he loves it, then it is someone who feels such loyalty and love for the Brotherhood that he is re-creating crimes in such a way to elevate the organization. Maybe warn others away from any negative comments, or from giving away its secrets."

Arden's eyes now came alive. "Good job, Charlie. I knew you'd get it."

She turned to Winston. "Don't you see? Don't you see what's happening? I don't know if it's coming from within the Brotherhood or not, but someone wants to make sure that old feelings re-emerge. Feelings that could cause the downfall of the Masons. They are using these symbols to make a point. Of all the conspiracy theories that exist, this is the easiest one to re-create. Everything is still here, down to the..." Her voice trailed off.

"Down to the what? You think that someone is out to destroy some cult, and in the process, destroy my theatre? This is ridiculous. I wish you luck in your witch hunt, Dr. James. I, meanwhile, must find my assistant and get him out of this mess. I have a theatre to run. Good day."

Winston stomped out as best he could. Arden and Charlie looked after him as he left.

"Down to the what?" asked Charlie.

"Down to the smallest detail. I think it is time to continue your tour of this brilliant city."

"Sounds good. Where, pray tell, are we going?"

"Pray tell? We are getting English now, aren't we? You'll be asking to meet the Queen next."

"Hey, if she wants to meet me, I wouldn't say no. I'm just impressed that you can recite a dissertation's worth of info off the top of your head."

"Yeah, well if you had spent as much time as I did researching this stuff - you kind of just learn it all."

"I'll remember that."

"You better. Come on. Let's go. I'm getting more and more curious to see what has been built up where that gatehouse was."

They walked out of the pub without noticing Peter leave his spot on the outside wall and continue to follow them. His foot still hurt from tripping on the steps a few minutes before and his eardrum ached from the earpiece that linked to the AV device in her pin. Managing to stay just within visual contact, all the while not letting them know he was there, had been the most difficult part, but thanks to a few different hats and newspapers, not impossible. It would have been much easier, of course, to use the video part of the pin, but that didn't always work well with the audio, and it was more important that he stay close and hear their conversations, then see exactly what was within eye level of the pin. He heard they were going to meet Winston at the Sussex in Leicester Square, and knew that Arden would take Charlie around to see some of the area first. He bypassed the two of them in the tube stop, and made his way to the pub. This had only given him a moment with the old man, but that was enough. It was time to clue Arden in on his whereabouts. He followed them towards the lodge, wondering what might be the best way to go about revealing himself.

## Chapter 24

**"Action is eloquence." - *Coriolanus***

Edward's day was now becoming truly terrible. After the two Americans ran off, he called Andrews, who had no news of Peter to share with him. Alec had come back though, babbling about the order, his Benefactor, and some other nonsense. As far as Edward was concerned, this type of behavior in public could only cause problems. Edward had cautioned Alec to go home and rest for a while. The last thing he needed was this cretin wandering around blathering secrets. Finally, he turned back to the task at hand: recasting the Porter.

His phone rang, breaking his concentration.

"Yes. Yes, I know what they think. Well, I'm not saying it's utterly far-fetched. Didn't you tell the old man to... Well, where are they now? Blast them. Well, they're not going to come back here, I'll tell you that much. Look, I have a show to save. I know how important this is. All right. Any news and I'll... Well, the show starts at 7:30... It's almost six now, and I don't have a damned Porter!"

He slammed the phone and turned to his assistant. "You're doing it."

"I'm what?" Miles was buried in a pile of headshots.

"It's one scene. You have an hour to learn your lines."

"I what?" Miles' jaw dropped, but no sound came out of his stunned mouth.

With that, Edward marched out of the room.

## Chapter 25

**"If music be the food of love, play on, Give me excess of it; that surfeiting,**

**The appetite may sicken, and so die." - *Twelfth Night***

The streets were getting darker. Thank God it was summer; they still had a few hours before the sun set completely. It was also getting late, and Arden had no idea if Edward would have sent someone out looking for them. For a long while, they were so deep in thought that neither Charlie nor Arden had any idea that twenty feet behind them, footprints echoed on the sidewalk. It was Charlie who noticed first. He stopped short and grabbed Arden.

"Don't say anything. Do you hear them?"

Confused, Arden shook her head. They kept walking. After a few steps, Arden heard them, too. The echoing grew louder, and Arden and Charlie sped up. Soon, they were running. The twisted streets of London flew out from under them. Charlie was just about to thank God that he had been on the track team when he tripped on a wet cobblestone. Damn, he thought. They didn't have cobblestones in the Maryland suburbs. Arden stopped to help him up, and before they could keep going, a voice from out of the shadows exclaimed, "'Ello, luv! Fancy this!"

Charlie had only heard that voice once before but recognized it immediately.

"Peter!" Arden exclaimed. "What are you doing here?"

"I might ask you the same question. I might, but I already know the answer."

"And that is..."

"You're lookin' for the Lodge. You won't find it. Not where you're lookin'. You might find somefink else, though. And fur that matter, luv, if you keep askin' the wrong people the wrong questions, you just might find yourself in worse trouble. I'm 'ere to help."

Peter smiled victoriously, and then turned to Charlie.

"I was wrong 'bout you, mate. I thought you were 'elping them. Seems you are just'is clueless as you seem t'be."

"What on earth do you mean?"

Peter checked his watch. "It'll be dark soon. No time to 'xplain now. I'll go with you lot to that old gatehouse. Er where it was anyway. We'll see what we find, and then while the show's 'appenin', we'll have a lit'l chat. Don't fink nothin' ll 'appen durin' the show. But we'd best be on the Southbank by the time it ends. It's *Macbeth* t'night."

"Peter, how on... how... what..."

"The gatehouse was just 'round that bend. Let's 'ave a look, yeah?"

They got within fifty feet of where the gatehouse was when Peter grabbed them and motioned for them to be quiet. Charlie, confused, noticed it first. A shadow. They hid in the corner, waiting to see if the shadow had seen them. They sneaked inside the closest pub and went over to the darkest corner possible. After they sat, Peter went to the bar and ordered a round of drinks.

"We'd best wait. No tellin' 'ow long he'll be there for. Care for a pint, lad?" Peter asked pushing the ale towards Charlie before waiting for a reply.

"This might be a good time for you to tell me what the hell is going on," Arden snapped.

"You might be right, luv. I hate to tell you this, but I was 'ssigned t'you. I fancied you, too, don't get me wrong, but me boss had me watchin' you." Peter slid a pint towards Arden too.

"You dated this guy?" Charlie exclaimed.

"Yeah. It's a long..." Arden's voice trailed off.

"Had a good time, didn't we? Great lit'l gal you've got yourself 'ere," Peter said.

"Oh, we're not—" But Charlie was interrupted before he could continue.

"Just tell me what this is about, Peter," Arden demanded.

"Well, a lit'l birdie told me about your research. A'tually, it told me boss. Me order's'er to keep'n eye on you. I was 'aving meself a grand ole time until you showed me your lit'l masterpiece. I knew then we was in for some trouble. I had t'get out of there. For your own good, luv. Me boss 'as been watchin' for a while. He got t'word a few years back that there was trouble brewin'. Seems some bloke was rejected from a position, as they wasn't the nicest of lads. Well, he was a bit miffed you might say, and wanted to get back at the buggers. At least that's what t'bloke Edward thinks."

"The director?"

"Yeah, you needn't 'ave run from him, lad. He's trying to 'elp you. He was helpin' us. Got me the job with the comp'ny so I could keep an eye on things. Everythink started comin' to a 'ead last year. Whoever this mean old bastard is that's killin' people waited and knew when the home office released the Ripper files. He's been studyin' them, y'see. Then we got word 'bout your work and I was assigned to you. After you published, a lad who worked for the Globe swiped a copy fur us to see. Which promp'ly got stolen."

"When did he swipe it? I didn't know it was missing until last night."

"Right after it made it to Paddy's office. That's what's so strange, yeah? Whoever swiped it from me must've been someone high enough in the Globe that knows your book was there t'swipe. The bastard's 'ad your book for a while. I took the book to me office, which's where it got pinched. So I think the wanker's in or got mates in Scotland Yard."

"Scotland Yard?"

"Yep. I've been doin' some undercover work, shall we say, for the coppers for 'bout eight years now." Peter took out a badge, which Arden examined closely.

"I'm on undercover work. I've been tracking this bloke since, oh, it's nearly five years now."

"Five years!"

"This buggers been savin' his energy. 'E's been waitin' to 'xplode, and now he 'as. We was 'fraid you were 'elping him, which you might have done, but not willingly. I didn't know meself 'till yest'rday, what would finally come about."

"I wasn't helping anyone kill anyone."

"I know that, luv," Peter softened. "The thing is, yeah, that y'did. You gave him a place to start, ya might say. All the symbols connectin' the Bard with the Freemasons... Gave 'im a perfect target. Or scapegoat, pendin' on 'ow ya look at it."

"What do we do now?"

"Just what you're doing. You shouldn't have talked to Paddy, though. Not real sure 'bout 'im."

"Do you think he has something to do with this?"

"Don't know, mate. There's a few of 'em we've been trackin'. Fact is, Paddy's an old codger who has too much at stake, Andrews says."

"What about Alec?" asked Charlie.

"Naw, too stupid. And he's a loyal Mason. Doesn't have an axe to grind."

"What about Andrews? Is there anything strange about him?"

"You crazy? That man'd do anythink t'stop this from 'appening. He's me boss. Been trying to 'ead it off this whole time. One step ahead of 'em. That's 'is way."

"Who then?"

"Good quest'n. If I knew the answer, this whole thing'd be done wivth. Now, if our mate in the shadows is still there, this party's gotta move back to the Globe."

"Do you think one of the actresses who plays the witches is next?" Arden looked intently at Peter.

"I'd say all three, t'be honest. It's just a matt'r of time. We're watchin 'em, we are. Gotta service t'night, and some of us coppers're over there t'protect 'em."

"So you know it's probably the witches who'll be targeted?" Charlie said suspiciously.

"Spot on, lad. I've been followin' you all day, I 'ave. Got a leg up on info, thanks to you. We know who the victims'll be, know where they'll be found—"

"Two questions," interrupted Arden. "Who is our Ripper, and how do we stop him?"

"Three questions," interjected Charlie. "You talked about hiding secrets. Secrets in a brotherhood hidden for decades. Does the new Ripper know who the first Ripper was?"

"Lad, 'ave you ever thought'f a career as a detective?" Peter smiled, downed his pint, and got up. Arden and Charlie began to follow.

"Nope. You lot stay 'ere."

"What?" Arden asked.

"For another five minutes. I'll check on our mate outside. If 'e's still there, I'll signal you from t'door.

"Signal us?" asked Arden. "How?"

Peter shook his head. "You'll know, luv. Look for't. If it's not there, go on and check out the Lodge. If it is, go to the Globe. I'll be followin' you. Don't want our friend to see me wivth you mates. I've spent a bit of me time in meetin's and those Masons are secret buggers. If our boy is one, or pretending to be one, he's goin't wonder what I'm doin' wivth you."

"Even if he's not, he'll wonder," Charlie said.

"Smart lad." Peter winked. "I'll find you at the theatre. By the gates near the water. At midnight. Cheers."

With that, Peter was gone.

## Chapter 26

**"I do love nothing in the world so well as you: is not that strange?"**

**- *Much Ado About Nothing***

"So, that was the guy?" Charlie asked when they were alone again.

"That was him." Arden seemed lost in thought for a minute. Then she suddenly turned to Charlie. "I sure know how to pick 'em, huh? Strike that. He picked me for an investigation. You'd think I would have learned sometime but he seemed so different."

"Just like Cassie."

"Yeah. I thought... well, shows what I know."

"I don't get it. Relationships, the whole thing. They suck," Charlie said.

"That's an understatement. I just wish..."

"I know."

Charlie took Arden's hand and smiled.

"It'll get better, you know," he said.

Arden returned the smile.

"It already has," she replied.

Charlie and Arden stared at each other. Charlie leaned in tentatively and kissed her softly. When he pulled back, she smiled. Chimes from a nearby church shook them out of their trance.

"We should look and see if the coast is clear."

"Yeah, you're probably right," Charlie said.

They crept towards the door in silence.

"I don't see anything. I guess it's safe to check it out."

"Wait, look..." The glow of the street lamps cast a dim glow on the thin layer of mist surrounding the stone walls, forming two human silhouettes. Charlie and Arden watched as the two shadows met each other. They could hear voices but couldn't make out what they were saying.

"Let's get closer," Charlie whispered.

Moving a bit more around the bend, they saw Peter speaking with someone whose back was to them.

"I've been looking for you. I had the other copy of the book; I didn't know what to do with it. And someone's dead. Did you know that? What the devil should I do?"

"Alec, old boy, calm yourself. Where'd ya take the book?"

"To him. The Grandmaster. I didn't mean to. I wasn't even supposed to. I was supposed to bring it to someone else, but I was looking for you, but you weren't at the meeting."

"Someone else? Who's that then?"

"Just someone. It's not important. What matters is that I don't have it anymore."

"It's all right, old boy. Nothin's gonna happen to it there. What I want't know, right, is what the bloody 'ell you're doin 'ere?"

"I have to be here. I'm performing a duty. Also, I was hoping you'd come by. I thought maybe you didn't know what time the meeting was, and I—"

"Perfomin' a duty? So who else knows you're'ere?"

"The people who should. That's all. It's no one else's business."

"Right then. Alec, mate, now, let me tell you what you're gonna do. You're gonna go 'ome, calm down, take a nice hot bath and put your feet up. Got that? It's all takin' care'f mate."

"But the American girl. She was looking—"

"I know. Don't you worry your pretty lit'l 'ead 'bout that. She's all right. She's got nothin' t'do wivth the murders."

"Murders? Plural?"

Peter sighed. "Alec, You've gotta trust me, yeah? Just go home and get some rest. It'll start rainin' soon, then you'll get yourself soaked if you stay out 'ere."

"But what do I do about Winston? The old codger won't stop ringing my mobile. And I can't leave. I told you. Not until I'm asked to."

Alec was not calming down. Peter had asked him for a copy of the book, and then it had turned up at a murder scene. On top of that, there was a second murder. Alec was protective of his brotherhood. Overly so, but he was still a coward. If people were dying, he didn't want anything to do with it. He got involved because he was asked to. He couldn't refuse his Benefactor. There was no turning back no matter how far along things went; although they were going a bit further than his comfort zone would allow.

"Peter, I'm scared," he said.

It took every ounce of willpower for Peter to remain calm. Breathe, he thought, I just have to breath. If things go wrong from here on out, it could be Arden's head. The thought of something happening to her roused Peter's determination to remain calm.

"Look," he said to Alec, "no one's commin' after you, yeah? Are you a prostitute? If ya are, I bloody well don't want t'know 'bout it. And last time I checked, you were a bloke, and ain't no one's after blokes. 'Less your name's Long Liz, or you're playin' a witch in *Macbeth*, no one's comin' after you. So let's go home, yeah? I'll take you there. By the way, I don't mean to change the subject or nothin', but is anyone else 'ere?"

"I haven't seen anyone I wasn't expecting. Just the fact that there is an emergency meeting that's been called. I told you I was on duty. I'm Tyler for the meeting. Don't look at me like that. It's a huge honor. This is a high level meeting, and they wanted me as guard."

Peter became uneasy. If Edward had called a meeting, he would have been told. The natural order seemed to be turning slowly on its head.

"Who called it?" Peter finally asked.

"I can't tell you that. Just... it's a small meeting. All I can say is they knew the knock, though, and were wearing robes by the time they got to me. Their faces were covered. That's all I can really say. They're inside."

"Well then, if anyone fancied havin' a look inside," Peter got really loud for a moment, "they'd better not."

"Shhhh, Peter, what's wrong?"

"Was I loud, luv? Fancy that. Well, better have a look at the door, just in case it's a meetin' I'd reckon I should be at, and then I'll walk you home."

Peter walked over to the door. He looked around and spotted Arden and Charlie smashed up against the wall of the opposite building. He looked at them and shook his head. They nodded and turned away. Peter made sure they were walking away from the gatehouse before looking at the door. There was the sign. An emergency meeting? But who? Granted, Peter was not really a Mason, but he knew that no meeting had been called. Edward had made a promise to let Peter know what was going on with the Brotherhood. He hadn't been too thrilled about it, as it was breaking a number of sacred oaths, but once presented with the facts, Edward had volunteered himself. As Grandmaster, it was his Brotherhood that was at stake.

"Fancy that," Peter murmured to himself. He turned back to where Alec had been standing. He was gone.

"Now where'd he go, then?"

Peter shrugged and walked around the side of the building to the back door. There was Alec, crouched along the side door.

"Are we going, then?"

"Not now, Peter. I can't, I have a job to do. Besides, I need time. I need to calm down. I'll go home soon, I promise."

"Suit yourself." Peter walked far enough away so that Alec couldn't see him and took out his mobile.

"Alec's at the meetin' house. He's playin' porter to someone whose havin' a meeting. No, I don't know who. If I did I reckon I'd tell you, Gov. Well, I'm not about to run off now. Yeah? I'll call if I find anything."

Peter hung up and sighed. As he did, it started to rain. "Blast," Peter heard himself say. This job was getting worse every minute.

## Chapter 27

**"Awake, dear heart, awake. Thou hast slept well. Awake." - *The Tempest***

Arden and Charlie had been walking for a while, huddled under Arden's umbrella in total silence. Charlie finally broke the audible void by attempting to synthesize what they had just heard. "Alec and Peter... what did they... Is that building—the one built where the old Gatehouse was—the meeting house?"

"I guess so. It's so strange because it's not the gatehouse anymore. The real gatehouse has been gone for some time. But that location... If it was a previous site of meetings, then it must have carried over. That definitely means that Shakespeare had Masonic connections. Otherwise, why would he have bought that floor of that specific building? He must have bought it for the Lodge. And that location is still a Masonic site."

"Are we meeting Peter later?"

"I don't see how we can help it. He's been following us for a while, I guess, and if we don't show up it could be bad."

"And his connection to Alec?"

"If he's been following the Masons as he said, then he must have befriended Alec. I mean, Alec does work at the Globe. He was probably instructed to in the same way that Peter was told to date me. Well, not quite the same I guess... I mean, Peter is a cop. Maybe Alec was brought into the Masons *because* he worked at the Globe? If someone wanted to have an inside look, Alec would be his man."

They kept walking. Finally, Charlie stopped at a bus stop that had an overhang and sat down on the dry bench. Arden looked at him.

"So," teased Charlie, "Peter was the guy you were talking about. Hmmm. Interesting taste, I must say."

"Yeah, yeah, yeah. Thanks for reminding me."

"Don't mention it. That's what I'm here for. Let's put it in perspective. How long were you together?"

"A few months. I really thought it would last, though. We had so much in common, and so much fun together..." She turned away, so Charlie couldn't see the tears welling up in her eyes.

He became serious for a moment. "I guess you never know about people."

"'There's no art to find the mind's construction in the face.' That's from *Macbeth.* Duncan says it before he's killed. It's true, though. You think you know people and then you find out your boyfriend's a cop who only dated you 'cause he thought you might be some psycho..."

"I like that quote. Come on. It could be worse. You could be running all over London trying to solve a copycat Jack the Ripper murder!"

"Yeah, imagine that."

Charlie smiled, "Well, here's to the broken-hearted. May we wallow in self-pity no longer."

"I agree."

"Let me think. Here's one. 'Every rose has its thorn.' Deep, huh?"

Arden laughed. "I like that one, too. 'And every dark has its dawn?'"

"'And every cowboy sings a sad, sad song.'"

"'Cause every rose has its thorn.'"

The world swelled around them. Lost in a cloud, the feelings became almost audible in their intensity.

Arden started laughing. "It's funny. I'm upset, but I could be much more so. I don't know, maybe I'm just distracted, but I don't feel as badly as I think I should."

"It's cuz I cheer you up."

"Oh, is that what you're doing? I wasn't sure."

"Hey, do you want me to tell jokes? I do that pretty well. Here's one: What do you call five rabbits jumping backwards?"

"What?"

"A receding hare line!"

"Ha, ha, ha. Very funny."

"Yeah, my dad hates that one. I've got plenty of others, though."

"I'd like to hear them. How about when this is all over, you tell me your jokes. We'll have a huge joke-telling bash."

Charlie got up and walked over to Arden. He looked deeply into her eyes, gave her a hug and said softly, "You've got a deal."

Arden's surprise consumed her. She liked this more than she should. It gave her enough of a start that after a bit she pulled away. Smiling, she said, "We better head on over. I think the show's about to begin."

They walked a little further as Arden struggled to unwrap her mind from Charlie's embrace. The Ripper, she thought to herself. The Masons. The intellectual's equivalent of a cold shower.

Finally, she spoke again. "You know, more than ever I don't think the original Ripper was backed by the Masons. He might have been a Mason, but if he was, I don't think the Brotherhood even knew about it until it was too late."

"And all these connections?"

"That's what's so weird. They are connections, but somehow, they feel wrong. Like one or two people misinterpreting something and coming up with an alternative universe. I mean, let's take it one at a time. If Walter Sickert, the painter, was the Ripper, then you can go with two different trains of thought. One, he was being bribed by someone to be involved because of Mary Kelly; or two, he was a stereotypical homicidal maniac. If it was George Chapman, or any of the people mentioned in some of the Polish Jew theories, then we've got something totally unrelated to this business.

"Come to think of it, you only relate it to the Masons if you go with the Stephen Knight conspiracy theory, or at least the basis of it. Well, and then there's the Prince Edward theory."

"And what's that one?" asked Charlie

"Well, that one intrigues me, and that one involves the Masons. That theory takes a few of the original suspects and turns the whole thing around. It's interesting... I mean it says Edward was having the affair, with Kelly as opposed to Annie Crook, and it was Kelly who got pregnant. To cover it up, a group of high-level Masons organized two men, J.K. Stephen, tutor to Prince Eddy, and Montague Druitt, another Ripper suspect, to kill Kelly and her confidants. But they killed Catherine Eddowes by mistake because she had used the name Mary Jane Kelly that night. When they realized the real one was alive, they went back and finished Mary Kelly off."

Arden paused for a moment before continuing.

"But there are so many other suspects who are completely unrelated. Do you know that people have actually written books that say Louis Carroll is the Ripper? They say that *Alice in Wonderland* actually contains hidden confessions from Carroll about the Ripper crimes."

"That's the dumbest thing I've heard in a while." Charlie shook his head.

"It's true, though. The book's called *Jack the Ripper, Light-Hearted Friend*. And Arthur Conan Doyle has been proposed as a suspect. Something to do with trying to stage a real-life Sherlock Holmes mystery."

"So basically, anyone alive in 1888 could be a suspect."

"Yep. Well, I think Oscar Wilde has been ruled out," Arden joked.

"How refreshing."

"Anyway, whoever's behind this is absolutely making a connection to the Knight theory, which has yet to be truly proven. Very few Ripperologists actually agree with Stephen Knight, but it is one of the more popular theories, and if anyone wanted to make connections with the Masons that could be understood by more than one or two people, that is the one they would go with."

Charlie shook his head. "It is amazing how much of that stream of consciousness I understood considering the fact that only yesterday 'the Ripper' could have been a heavy metal band or a name of a paper shredder."

Arden smiled. "Well, at least I'm educating you."

"Who is George Chapman? And what are the Polish Jew theories?"

"Those are just other theories. Detective Aberline who investigated the case believed the Ripper was a Russian man named George Chapman. The overall attitude at the time was, 'Oh, it can't be an Englishman, it must be a foreigner,' and many witnesses said they saw a foreign-looking man talking to the victims. Hence, there are theories about a variety of Polish Jews that lived in the area at the time. There is a lot more to it, but it's not important."

"Of course not. I think I got it, though. Polish Jew. Ya know, I'm a Polish Jew."

"So am I. Fourth generation American."

"As far as I know, no serial killing tendencies. You?

"Nope, not a one."

Almost by accident, they realized that they had walked the whole length of the bridge and the untamed streets of Southwark. It came as a complete surprise to find themselves standing in front of the Globe Theatre. They bought tickets—second balcony near the stage, to get an overall view in case anything strange happened—and went inside.

"And if anything strange does happen, what exactly are we supposed to do?" asked Charlie.

"I suppose it depends on what that strange thing actually is," Arden whispered.

They sat down and about two minutes later focused their attention on the stage. About two hours later, somewhere in the groundlings, a shaken Peter arrived just in time to see Macbeth defeated by Macduff.

## Chapter 28

**"Virtue is bold, and goodness never fearful." - *Measure for Measure***

Peter had not had an easy time sniffing around the lodge. Alec had definitely been vigilant in playing the role of Tyler or Porter for this important meeting. It had seemed like ages before two hooded figures left the building. They thanked Alec and discharged him from his post. Unable to make out faces due to heavy black cloaks and turned backs, Peter decided to search the abandoned building instead of following either of the two men as they had left in different directions, and there was no point in trying to decide which to follow.

The meetinghouse was locked, but Peter let himself in through a secret side door. Thank the Lord these old buildings had so many secret passages. He would have entered sooner, while the meeting was on, but Alec had kept circling the building and the door squeaked loudly. Secret indeed. One day someone would use it during a meeting, everyone would hear a distorted thud against the stonework, and that would be the end of the secret.

The flames from the torches were smoldering from recent usage, filling the air with a smoky haze. Peter made his way, the narrow corridor lit only by the thin beam of his flashlight. Nothing seemed out of place. Peter arced his light around and was just about to leave when he noticed a handkerchief lying in front of a wall. He looked closer at the handkerchief and then looked at the wall itself. He had been in this room many times in the last two years masquerading as a Mason and never thought anything of most of the space. He recoiled a little when he realized that this section of wall had the faint outline of a door. Another secret passage! He pushed gently at first, then harder. The door began to open, and Peter entered another long dark hallway.

He walked for what seemed like ages. The air that filled his senses was thick with moisture and the pungent odors from centuries of use. He finally came to a set of doors that opened into a cavernous room filled with bookcases. In the middle of the room was a single massive wooden table with equally massive wooden chairs. Looking around, Peter realized that every possible bit of wall space was covered with shelves holding a plethora of cardboard files and glass jars. Peter walked in slowly, allowing his nose to adapt to the smells emanating from the mysterious containers. They were all labeled. Peter crept over and perused some of the files.

"Blimey!"

Startled by the sound of his own surprise, Peter looked around anxiously. After a shaky moment, he turned back to the files.

There were hundreds of them. Each file was labeled with old names, important names, and each jar contained distorted masses of eerie centuries-old relics. The glare of the flashlight rested on a section labeled "Ripper." Each suspect had a file. People who weren't suspects had files. Strangely enough, various Masons from different historical periods had their files placed in the Ripper section. All the key players of Shakespeare's day were carefully catalogued and interspersed among prominent Victorians.

They were all there, in alphabetical order, and ranged from Fludd, the Rosicrucian Priory leader, to Sir William Gull and Prince Eddy. Each Ripper victim had her own file as well. Peter misjudged the corner of the table as he traversed across the room.

"Blast!"

Bending over to curse both the table and his sore knee, the light found some white documents close to the offending corner. One file was laid out, opened on the table.

*Huh*, thought Peter. *Well, here's a pretty mess of things. I suppose it wants me to read it. It wouldn't be here otherwise*. The name on the file read "Francis Tumblety/Thompson." He leafed through it... slowly at first, but then faster and with greater interest. After reading it, an amazed Peter took an article out, folded it and stuffed it in his jacket.

Suddenly, he heard a train roll by... really close by. Peter walked slowly to the side of the room where he had heard the train. He opened the door and took a step back, startled. He was standing right next to underground tracks. In fact, there was an underground platform right in front of him, and on the platform, there was a flag on the wall folded down. He pushed it up, setting off a strange blue light on the side of the platform. He waited for a moment in utter curiosity. Sure enough, the next train that came by stopped for him. He got in with the driver, and three minutes later they were across the bridge and at the London Bridge tube stop.

Peter left the train and when he was above ground, opened his mobile. “Yeah, Gov? I got some interesting news for you.” After a few minutes, Peter was on his way to the Globe Theatre.

## Chapter 29

**"Make use of time, let not advantage slip." - *Venus and Adonis***

When the show had played out, Charlie and Arden decided to head over to The George before meeting Peter. They were deep in conversation.

"No, I've never seen it before. I mean I have read it in class, but I think I didn't pay attention. I didn't know that Macbeth killed Macduff's whole family," Charlie explained.

"Yep, every last one. Mostly out of fear and panic, in my opinion. I loved the woman who played Lady Macbeth, though. She was awesome."

"And completely psycho."

"Yeah, but she's supposed to be. She's the reason why Macbeth actually goes through with it."

"Well, I hope I never date a girl like that."

"I don't think anyone is really like that. Or at least I hope not." She paused. "What kind of girl do you want to date?"

"You. Someone smart, pretty, someone who gets my sense of humor. Someone I can love and do nice things for without her walking all over me. That would be nice." Arden laughed and Charlie wasn't sure if she was ignoring his opening line on purpose.

"I bet you make a really great boyfriend."

"I like to think I do. Just... I keep getting, I don't know, trampled on. Cassie, for instance, did not appreciate the things I did for her."

"Obviously not if she cheated on you."

"Yeah, but even before that, I don't know. We had broken up a few times, and I tried to do all these nice things for her. She kept running away from me."

"What kind of nice things?"

"Well, there was the time I went to her house and put flowers on her pillow... I made her collages with songs I had written... I don't know, just nice things."

"And she didn't appreciate it? I've never had anyone stop by my house just to put flowers on my pillow!"

"Yeah, well, I'm just a sucker for romance. She didn't seem to care, anyway. My friends told me to break up with her for good, but I just couldn't. There was just something about her. I thought I loved her."

"I thought I loved Peter. I thought I had it all figured out."

"I don't know if there's such a thing as figuring it all out."

Peter's voice scared them out of their thoughts. "Figure out what, luv?"

"Peter!" Arden exclaimed. "It's not nice to sneak up on people like that. And what are you doing here? I thought we were meeting you later?"

"Ah, that's somethin' I'm good at. Surprisin' people. Had a bit of a surprise meself not too long ago."

"Anything worth mentioning? Relevant to this, I mean?" Arden hissed.

"Well, I did 'ave me a bit of important information you might say, and although you lot were not s'pposed to find me for another hour or so, I thought to meself, there's really no reason to beat around the bush, so I made me mind up to check and see if you lot were 'ere. Arden, you are a lovely girl, but far too predictable you might say."

"Charlie, next time I suggest The George, remind me to change my mind."

"Sounds like a plan," Charlie replied.

"Anyway, Peter, what have you got for us?" Arden asked.

"My lit'l Ripperologist. Have you ever heard of a suspect named Francis Tumblety? Or Thompson?"

"Yeah, they are two different people. Francis Tumblety was a mad doctor. An American actually, who fled back home after the murders. Scotland Yard detectives followed him. He is still considered one of the most viable suspects. Francis Thompson was different. I've come across his name on various suspect lists. He was a zealous Christian, and thought he was St. Francis. Not much else."

"D'you read a casebook website?"

"I have, yes. It's a valuable resource. I've gotten tons of information from it and been referred to it by some of the books I have. Why?"

"Well, I have an article 'ere that might make you change your mind. Seems Francis, the Thompson one, failed in everythink he did. Went to priest school, failed that. Went to med school, failed that too. Studied to become a surgeon in fact. Also a religious zealot. Begged around London fur a few years."

"I guess that's what makes him a viable Ripper suspect," Arden replied. "I don't see him as being the Ripper, though. Why?"

"Well, this here article talks about some religious stuff that might be right up your alley, yeah?" Peter handed Arden the folded piece of paper and pointed to a spot for her to start reading. Charlie saw Arden turn pale as she read.

"What is it?" Charlie asked.

She began reading, "'The first murder, that of Mary Ann (Polly) Nichols, occurred on August 31st. In the Catholic calendar of patron saints, this date falls upon the feast day of Saint Raymond. The patron saint of innocence.

"'This 13th century Cardinal was also the patron saint of midwives, childbirth, children, and pregnant women. Saint Raymond was a missionary who was imprisoned by Muslims in Algeria for attempting to convert the poor. His lips were pierced and his mouth was shut up with a padlock. The lock was only removed when he ate. After being freed, Saint Raymond insisted on traveling as a peasant, in which manner he died on his way to visit the Pope.

"'The second murder, of Annie Chapman, occurred on September the 8th. This date falls on the feast day of Saint Adrian. This saint was an imperial officer who made himself a Christian before he was baptized. He was imprisoned for this and was then martyred by being thrown into a furnace. His wife kept his hand. Saint Adrian is the patron saint of Soldiers and Butchers. He lived in the East.

"'The night of the double murders, upon which Elizabeth Stride and Catherine Eddowes were killed, occurred on September the 30th. This falls on the feast day of Saint Jerome. This saint was a scholar who settled in the eastern city of Bethlehem and was known for his short temper. He is the Patron saint of Doctors and Scholars. Saint Jerome translated the Bible into a Latin work known as the Vulgate.

"'The last murder, that of Mary Kelly, occurred on November the 9th. This fell on the feast day of Saint Theodore. This saint was a Roman soldier who, after setting fire to a temple, was tortured. In prison Saint Theodore saw visions and was martyred by being thrown into a furnace. He was known as one of the great 'soldier saints' of the Eastern Orthodox Church. Said to have battled a dragon, Saint Theodore is their Patron saint of Soldiers.

"'One possible motive for the Ripper to have killed these five women, and then send letters to the press, was that he thought that he had been chosen by God and that he was the voice of God. Perhaps by killing these five women, he would be inflicting five wounds upon society's church, government, science, literature, and people.

"'Perhaps Jack the Ripper perceived himself as a 'messiah' who, by killing within a religious site in London's east upon the feast days of martyred saints, could sin and be forgiven. These saints were all eastern crusaders, and patron saints of Innocence, Butchers, Soldiers, Doctors, and Scholars. The Ripper may have attempted to simulate the key concepts of the original crucifixion. Perhaps by killing five perceived 'sinners,' Jack the Ripper was attempting to project the five wounds of Christ's crucifixion onto a stigmata of immediate social impact. And thus, as a crusading knight, Jack the Ripper could elect himself a key player in an apocalypse and be forgiven of his sins.'"

Arden stopped reading. "There's the connection. I can't believe it! It's been there the whole time! I can't believe I never notices the specific significance of the dates!"

Charlie felt confused and relieved at the same time. "Are you saying one of these Francis guys was the Ripper?"

"No, I'm not, this hardly proves that—about either of them. It's the dates that are important. I didn't know that there was any significance to the specific dates of the murders. It goes along with the idea that there was a finger being pointed by someone to the Masons, but in the wrong way. See, what it does create is a connection between the victims and specific Christian symbols. The Knights were bound originally to protect the temple in the east during the Crusades. The dates of the murders connect the east to the west so to speak. If anything, this proves that the Masons themselves wouldn't have been connected to the murders. The Masons are not a religious organization. They allow freedom of religion because of the persecution of the Knights by the Pope. However, if someone who was religious wanted to make a statement, then these saints and these dates would do just that. Wow. This could be the missing link."

"Now 'old on," said Peter. "Are you saying this does not connect the Masons to this crime?"

"Well, it connects the Knights to the killings in the sense that someone who vaguely knew the history of the Knights, someone who wanted to make a statement in their own right, and someone who acted without the blessing of the organization acted in the name of his own religion, maybe even thinking that he was doing it for the Brotherhood. Sir Charles Warren must have made the association when the murderer left the message on the wall, but then it either took time to figure out who exactly was responsible, or nothing could be done for some reason until after Mary Kelly was killed. That would explain it."

"What message?" Charlie asked.

"There was a message left after the double murder that read, 'the Juwes are the ones who will not be blamed for nothing.' Juwes spelt J-U-W-E-S. The message was erased before it could be photographed, but the people who killed Hiram Abiff—the legendary architect of the Temple of Solomon—were Jubello, Jubella, and Jubellum. Someone in Whitechapel with enough education to read and write well enough to create the writing on the wall would probably have known how to spell *Jew*, so it is thought by some that he was referring to someone else. He could have been talking about Jews, but then he should have spelled it right.

"The freaky part was why the writing was erased so quickly. Also, it wasn't allowed to be photographed because Charles Warren, the Police Commissioner in charge of the investigation, who was a Mason, showed up and insisted it be erased. He said it was to protect the Jews in the area, but he also allegedly had the one photograph that had been taken of it destroyed. Because it was erased, records of the message tend to vary slightly. However, the widely agreed-upon correct message was, 'The Juwes are the ones who will not be blamed for nothing.' This lends support to the Mason conspiracy theory, but it also could have been that Warren saw the writing, realized that his Brotherhood was either involved, accused, or falsely implicated, and had it erased in order to protect one of his own, so to speak. The other thing is, in the story of Hiram Abiff, all three 'Juwes' together are actually referred to as 'the Juwe.' If the original Ripper was a Mason, he would not have put an 's' at the end."

"I think I'm following. But I thought you said someone named Anderson was the Police Commissioner."

"He was the Assistant Police Commissioner. And what is also funny is Warren resigned as commissioner the day of the Mary Kelly murder."

"Right, then, lad, I'm glad you're followin', 'cause I'm not," said Peter. "Arden, is this or isn't this the connection we're after?"

"It could be. I mean, I'm positive that although it seems like it implicates the Masons, it actually points away from the organization at the time, and the organization as a whole today for that matter. But if there are people today, or back then for that matter, who feel they have a divine right to make some statement... who don't fully understand, or misunderstand, then this does absolutely establish a connection, in a symbolic sense, with the murders."

"Ah, then that's what's doing." Peter shook his head.

Arden sighed. "Okay, here's an example. The Masons are a brotherhood that was founded for a purpose. The Templar Knights had a specific function. They had to protect a secret. It was a secret so important that all rules were established to ensure its survival. Then the organization was destroyed and went underground. Now, not only were they protecting the secret of the Grail, but also the lives of the Knights themselves. More rules were established, and the penalties were real—being discovered meant death. The organization evolved, eventually becoming the Masons, which came out publicly in 1717.

"Once the Organization went public, the rules no longer functioned to keep these people alive, and the initial Grail secret was long buried. In addition, the Brotherhood splintered. As some members moved to America, Freemasonry began to take on different forms. One branch of Masonry even broke off and eventually became the KKK. Another branch became the Golden Dawn, and a third became the Shriners. Their traditions evolved from the original organization but mutated to serve new functions. British Freemasonry evolved differently from American Freemasonry. An example is the fact that the rituals associated with the building of the temple and Hiram Abiff were removed from British Freemasonry but remained intact in America. By the time of the Ripper murders, the oaths had been filtered from most British lodges. However, no matter which school of thought you follow, the need for a secret society that allowed religious freedom was hardly the same as it had been a few hundred years earlier. Individuals reciting oaths and following rules had more room to devise their own interpretations. Therefore, a religious person, whether they were a member or not, might assign their religious beliefs to a completely non-secular brotherhood. Do you understand?"

"Let me get this straight." Charlie was desperately filtering the information. "Jack the Ripper of 1888 might have been a person who wasn't a Mason but wanted to be or knew something about them. Someone who thought the Masons were religious and had read all about these rituals. Am I following so far?"

"Yup. Go on."

"And that person wanted to implicate the Masons for some reason but did it wrong."

"Exactly."

"But this person, our twenty-first century Jack, is probably a Mason, who *is* religious, who misunderstands what the Brotherhood is about and what the original crimes were about?"

"Yes. Exactly!"

Peter looked at her sideways. "Are you sure? I think you've gone off your rocker, you have."

"Thank you, Peter," Arden said wryly, raising an eyebrow. "I know what I'm saying, whether you believe me or not."

"Hey, Peter," began Charlie, "where did you find this paper?"

"That, my dear boy is too hard to 'xplain. Would you like me t'show you?"

"Do we dare say no?"

"You lot have to come wiv me if ya don't mind."

"Where are we going?"

"To the London Bridge tube stop."

**Chapter 30**

**"Look, he's winding up the watch of his wit; by and by it will strike." - *The Tempest***

The Benefactor followed Peter as far as The George Inn. He had work to do, and he couldn't spend all day following up on this strange new development. Stupid Americans. They always got in the way. This one was smart, too. And who was the Brit following them around? This was also unexpected. He hated the unexpected when it happened to him. But these people were not smart enough to get anywhere close to where he was. Certainly, Arden was brighter than he had given her credit for, but she couldn't possibly understand.

"Americans," he sighed. He took out his mobile. Alec was a fool, but a fool who would do what he was told. He dialed the number.

"Alec. I have an important assignment for you.... Yes, I know about them. That is not your concern. Calm down, my brother. Just follow my directions."

On the other end of the line, Alec listened carefully to his instructions.

"All right. I'm off then," Alec replied. He hung up and headed back towards the warehouse where the whole cast of *Macbeth* had assembled for a mourning session and memorial service. That was unimportant. The only focus was who would be there, and what he was supposed to do with them.

## Chapter 31

**"Some are born great, some achieve greatness, and some have greatness thrust upon them." - *Twelfth Night***

Peter left them on the platform to speak with a manager. A few minutes later, they got into the driver's seat of a train and rode to what seemed like a hole in a wall. They got off and lingered on the makeshift platform as the train drove away.

"Where are we?" Charlie asked.

"This, my friends, is the back exit, so to speak, of the meeting house. Found it meself about three hours ago. Follow me, and you best hold your nose 'till you've gotten yourself used to it."

Arden and Charlie crept behind Peter as he walked back through the corridor to the secret room. When they arrived, Peter shined his flashlight at the table and gasped.

"What's wrong?" Arden whispered.

"This... the files..." Peter stared in amazement. All the files were as they should be, but the folder that he had left out on the desk was gone. He looked on the wall and saw that it had been neatly put away. "The paper I gave you was from a file that was all thrown on this table. Someone's been here after me, put it all away."

"This is crazy," Charlie said, looking at some of the names. "There's a file here on George Washington, Thomas Jefferson, and well, just about everyone."

He was right; there were hundreds if not thousands of files all over the room.

"Well, whoever it is isn't around now," Arden whispered nervously.

"I'd better check. I'll be a few. It's a long walk to the gatehouse that," said Peter.

"This leads to the gatehouse?" Arden gasped.

"Yup. Seems our friends have a convenient way of gettin' to and from Southwark without no one knowing." He took out matches and lit the candles that were placed around the table. Then he took his flashlight and crept through the corridor towards the lodge.

"That's amazing," Arden said.

"How long do you think this has been here?" Charlie asked.

Arden looked at the files. Some were antique. The jars themselves could have been the primary display in a 'Containers Through the Ages' exhibit at a museum. As things got older, the shapes changed. Some had been put in plastic to be preserved better. Some documents had recently been put in clear plastic folders. The oldest looking documents were in protective cases, and the whole room reminded Arden of the creepy, smelly old basement of her college library.

"It looks as though records have been kept here for hundreds of years. Probably since the gatehouse was built. It's a big room. I think it was meant to be a library of some kind. Like a secret archive."

"How is that possible?" asked Charlie.

"The Blackfriars Gatehouse was allegedly used to smuggle priests out of nearby Catholic homes during the Reformation. However, the London Bridge Gatehouse would have technically helped regulate activity on the bridge. Before the tube was built, the tunnel probably led out to London Bridge itself. It was a busy enough bridge with houses and heavy foot traffic. I bet someone could have gone in and out of either without anyone thinking twice about it. The gatehouses were pretty far apart, if you were walking. The streets are hardly a straight line. This basically connects the bridge and the city. In fact, keeping the archives here would probably guarantee that in case of a raid on the lodge, their files would still be kept safe and hidden. It makes Shakespeare's purchase even more significant because this location has obviously been in use for hundreds of years. I'm impressed at the condition of everything. It's amazing this room wasn't destroyed in a fire or bombed out during the war."

Charlie was looking though a few of the files.

"This is amazing. All these people were Masons?"

"I don't know. Most of them were, but some of these Ripper folders..."

Arden picked up the one, labeled *George Chapman*. "He wasn't a Mason... and these articles are recent." She took out the *Druitt* folder. It was much older and had notes scribbled on yellowed paper that had been put in plastic, as well as articles as recent as a few weeks ago. In fact, all the people who had been suspects in the original investigation had old folders, full of similar hand-written notes as well as printouts from the Internet. Suspects whose popularity had begun recently only had new files.

"Someone followed the case really closely a hundred years ago, but then someone else went through them recently and added a mass of modern-day theories and research. Look! My book is here! My Ripper book!"

In a box labeled 'RIPLIT: Assorted documents,' Arden dug out her book, along with new editions of other Ripper books.

"RipLit. That's funny," Charlie said. "At least this creep has a sense of humor."

"Look, this one has cut outs from old newspapers... *'General Times—Leather Apron.'*"

Arden flipped through a scrapbook of newspaper clippings.

"This is interesting; the older articles stop. The last cutout is from January 30, 1889."

"Who or what is Leather Apron?" Charlie asked.

"That was what they first called Jack the Ripper."

"Why?"

"A number of reasons. They found a leather apron near one of the crime scenes. It was covered with blood. Also, butchers wore leather aprons. They even arrested a suspect who was later exonerated, who was known in the east end as Leather Apron. He had been hiding at his brother's house the night of the second murder because after the Nichols murder, women had accused him of being the killer. He freaked out and hid."

"Huh. So, whoever it was in 1889, stopped cutting out articles."

Arden peered closer at the files. "This is strange. The articles are cut and neatly placed in here for a while, but then after November 10, 1888, some articles are ripped out, and shoved in... and then they stop. The next thing in here is a Xerox of an archived web review for a 1970's BBC movie. Then there are loads of modern articles. I'd say almost the whole casebook by the look of it. It's like the Ripper kept tabs on himself, then someone else kept tabs on him, then he was forgotten until..."

Her voice trailed off. They looked at each other and silently continued going through files.

Meanwhile, Peter crept through the tunnel towards the lodge. As he got closer, he began hearing voices. Peter turned off his flashlight and continued moving towards the door until he could make out what was being said.

"Thank you for coming, sir. I'm terribly sorry to bother you, but it is quite important."

Peter recognized Alec's voice at once. What the devil was he doing there?

"It had better be. I was in the middle of an exceptionally important engagement."

The voice was gruff and cold. It was one that Peter did not recognize.

"Yes, sir, but it seems that someone has violated the Lodge."

"Pardon?"

"I came in here to lock up after the emergency meeting, and the hidden door, sir. It was open."

"Was anything out of place?"

"No, sir, not that I could tell. But then I went to the archive room, and there was one file which... It was on the table, and there was a document missing from it."

"What do you mean, missing?" The voice hissed angrily.

There was silence while Alec summoned up his remaining courage.

"I mean, sir, there is a page missing. I cleaned it up and put it away, after looking all over the room for it. I think someone snuck in and desecrated the lodge by stealing one of our documents."

On the side of the wall that Peter was not on, the gruff man, the lodge historian, Billingsworth, upset that he had been pulled out of an important dinner engagement, noticed a strange shadow. The door to the corridor had not been pulled tight when Alec, in his haste, had called the old archivist. As Alec rambled on, Billingsworth walked slowly towards the door. In one swift motion, before Alec was even done speaking, Billingsworth pushed the door open, exposing Peter who, taken by surprise, was standing right there, holding his flashlight.

"Brother Peter. Please. Join our conversation. Perhaps you know something about this so-called desecration."

"Peter!" Alec exclaimed. "What, why... Did you... You aren't supposed to know about this!"

Peter, having recovered from the shock of being discovered, quickly began accounting for himself. "What, mate? An' how d'you know what I am 'sposed to know? I didn't know *you* knew about it. Fancy that. I'm 'ere, doin' the job that's asked of me, and I hear voices in the Lodge, ones that I know meself shouldn't be here, and what d'you know."

Alec looked strangely at Peter. Billingsworth, however, did not seem surprised. "Yes, well, seems the mystery's been cleared up. Listen, lad, I'll have a walk down with you back to the Archives. Just to make sure you don't have any questions, of course. Thank you, Alec, for the brilliant interruption to my evening. I believe your job as Porter is now complete. You may go."

With that, Billingsworth came inside the corridor with Peter, pulling out his own flashlight. He shut the door tightly behind him, leaving a startled Alec with nothing to do but go back to the outside world. When Alec got there, he pulled out his mobile.

"He's there. Sir, I wonder... Yes. I know. Right. I'm on my way. Yes, sir."

With that Alec started to make his way to his Benefactor.

**Chapter 32**

**"What is he that builds stronger than either Mason?" - *Henry V***

They walked through the tunnel towards the room. When they were a safe distance from the Lodge, Billingsworth stopped walking. He was a big man, and he had been in charge of the archives for many years. There were guesses as far as his age was concerned. No one actually guessed correctly, but since he bragged about his friendship with Winston Churchill, the man was no youngster. He knew everything. It was his job. He had known everything for years and was not about to stop. He was the only other Mason besides the Grandmaster, as Peter thought, that knew Peter was not a Mason. However, until this moment, Billingsworth had not known what Peter was actually doing as part of the Lodge.

"You're a copper, aren't you?"

Peter nodded.

"I thought so. Wouldn't make sense any other way." He began walking again.

"Look, Billingsworth—" began Peter.

"You got friends down there in the archives don't you, lad?"

"How did...?"

"I see the lights there. Pokin' about for information. Well, I wondered when all this would come about."

"All what?"

"Introduce me to your mates, lad."

The sight of Billingsworth approaching with Peter was enough to scare the daylights out of Charlie and Arden.

"It's all right, mates," Peter said. "This 'ere's Billingsworth. He's keeper of the archives. Knows everything, he does. Maybe he can answer some of your questions."

"Hello, I'm Arden, this is Charlie... We are... um—"

"Trying to solve a murder, are you?"

They all stared at him in disbelief.

"Nothing gets past me, my dear. I've been here since long before you both were born, and I've seen just about everything. This is stranger than usual, granted, but not too strange for me to not understand."

"What can you tell me about Jack the Ripper, sir?" Arden asked.

Billingsworth sighed and sat down. "Better make yourself comfortable."

They all sat down around the table. Billingsworth cleared his throat. "Right. Well, first off, the Ripper was not a Mason. Oh, he wanted to be, and tried to prove to everyone that he could be and should be. Even took up with one of the brothers. A rather high-profile one. Can't tell you who, of course. But our Ripper lad, he studied everything that went on. He somehow hid in this corridor during meetings and rituals to know everything he could about our ways. In the Summer of '88, he was told by the Grandmaster at the time that he was not invited to join and needed to—how shall I put it—sod off.

"Our boyo was more than disappointed. He'd heard quite a bit while nosing around. Knew too much. There were dealings with the east end that had been covered up with the greatest care. However, our lad was not about to let them lie. He learned of them dishonestly, and in the same way, he took to trying to, well, point them out. Rumor has it that he even tried blackmail to become a brother. Of course, that didn't work. The Grandmaster was ardent. No one who was of so low a character was worthy of membership. That part is legend. The real motives are, of course, a matter of the greatest secrecy.

"Our lad then decided to get together with yet another mate, who was not a Brother, to prove his worth, so to speak. The result... Jack the Ripper. His first mate—the one who was a Mason—kept tabs on the killings. Hid them in the archives with all the other files. Figured no one would notice. That wasn't the case. My granddad was the archivist then, and he was updating the index when he came across the hidden files. He reported this at once and an investigation began within the organization. It was kept quiet in order to catch the scoundrel red-handed. It didn't stay as quiet as it should've, mostly due to the fact that our Ripper used bits and pieces of ritual to point blame at the Brotherhood. He didn't mean that, of course. He meant to leave clues so as to be deemed worthy or knowledgeable."

"Like the message? About the Juwes?"

"Yes, my dear. Only nothing was... how shall I put it...?"

"Quite right? I mean, things were slightly off," Arden interjected.

"Yes indeed. After Mary Kelly, the investigation became quite heated. It had become more intense with the other killings, but after that Kelly girl was taken apart, poor soul, the pitch reached an unheard-of furor. See how these articles are torn out? Our boy had stopped helping his mate. He'd been disgusted, and his mate became sloppy. Our Ripper lad was sneaking in on his own to add to what he considered his greatest achievement. He'd also gotten sloppy. Anyone with half a brain would have stopped coming down here. But not him. He was caught one night, and the whole affair was covered up and halted."

"Did your grandfather tell you who the Ripper was?" Arden asked eagerly.

"Nope. Wasn't the sort to say too much. Wasn't about to betray any brother, no matter what the bastard was doing."

"What about the guys who weren't brothers?" asked Charlie.

"Didn't tell me their names either. Felt that as keeper, I should know about what happened, but not who did it so to speak. Had good reason, too. The whole affair was hushed up, but it sent the Lodge into a state of absolute madness. Everyone felt betrayed, not to mention terrified. We are a private brotherhood. Our affairs must never be revealed. Luckily, the men did not know enough, or rather did not understand correctly, as you said. That's why in these recent murders, things were not quite spot on. For example, the re-enactments did not follow the murders as he thought they would."

"Like the wrong shoulder," Arden interrupted again.

"You've done your homework, young lady. Exactly. The brother who helped him was not the most observant lad in the world, and little details such as the right versus left shoulder escaped him. The choice of days was daft, as well. He meant them to be important, but all they did was reflect his own religious piety. He missed the important bits, and..."

"The eastern connection to the original Knights," Arden finished.

"Well, my child. I'm impressed."

"What happened to them?"

"My granddad said was that it was dealt with."

"Did he tell you anything else?"

After a beat, he replied, "Child, it's my job to know things like this, as it will be the job of the next archive keeper. One must keep the knowledge alive you know. History is history."

Billingsworth sighed and looked towards his files. "There are some things that are hidden in these pages still. I shouldn't worry too much. One day the truth will come out; names will be revealed. It is inevitable. Until then, it's my job to keep them clean, protected, and most importantly, out of public circulation."

"And this new Ripper?" Arden asked.

"Ah yes, the two murders. Yes, I know about the other one. Edward told me after it happened. He asked me to see what I could dig up. Any links," Billingsworth laughed. "Any links. All the links. To the wrong things, mind you. Whoever this bugger is, he knows about our lad. He knows, but, like the misguided predecessor, he does not understand. He doesn't understand the Brotherhood or the first lad's intentions. He does not know the real story. He's putting the Brotherhood in danger and he doesn't even understand why."

"What do you know about the Shakespeare connection?" Arden was fascinated now.

"Shakespeare. Yes. I have some theories. It all boils down to convenience. The Brotherhood is the connection. So far as I can figure, he's using all the Freemason symbols in Shakespeare to point a finger towards our Brotherhood."

Charlie decided it was his turn to chime in. "Do you think a Brother would really do that? I mean, what if it's like before? Someone who was jilted and wants to get even. Someone who is using these symbols to make a connection that doesn't actually exist?"

"I suppose it's possible. I'll tell you, lad, I've been going over this whole thing, and I hit a wall every time. I don't know anyone who'd want to do that. The only one I can think of..."

Billingsworth stopped short and thought for a moment. "There was one bugger. Kept poking around the Lodge. Years ago, now. He was not invited to be a member and was mighty disappointed, as his mate was a Brother. Can't remember his name, don't think I ever knew it, to be honest. His mate's a chap named Hendry."

"The professor?" Arden exclaimed.

"Yes, that's the one."

"He's the one who's your boss, I reckon, Arden," Peter said.

Arden nodded.

"He's a Brother, but he had a friend who wasn't?"

"Yes. But again, that was years ago. The boy hasn't been seen round here since."

Arden sighed. "I don't know if that rules anyone out. I mean, at this point, anything is possible."

"Heya, what 'bout Alec?" Peter asked. "Why was he pokin' around 'ere?"

"Alec was here?" Charlie asked.

"Yup, scared me stupid to see 'em. Was with Billingsworth in the Lodge."

"I received a call earlier, when they had that meeting, and they told me Alec would be here doing some research for him," Billingsworth said. "Then Alec rang, urging me to meet him here. It was a rather inconvenient call, but I do have a duty."

"Who called you earlier to tell you about the meeting?" asked Arden.

"Didn't say. He spoke in code."

"Code?"

"If a Brother needs to use the archives, they let me know. Procedure. They don't have to tell me who they are, there's a code. That tells me it really is a Brother. I don't ask why. They have their reasons. I usually find them out anyway. Something's always amiss in the files after they've been looked through. It's my job to clean up."

"There was a file out when I got 'ere before," Peter said. "Took this from it." He handed Billingsworth the folded piece of paper.

"Ah, yes. That's what Alec was on about. Well, I'm glad to see that nothing was desecrated, as he feared. There have been lots of strange things that seem to suddenly be popping up in the Ripper files. New files, as well. As a rule, I don't keep records on people who aren't Brothers."

"All these Ripper suspects weren't brothers. And some of these files are new," Arden pointed to two different piles of folders.

"Yes, well, you see, I didn't put them there." Billingsworth became grim. He looked intently at Arden. "Our friend Peter here was introduced to me by the Grandmaster. What he might not know is that it is because of me that he is here."

"What'd you mean?" asked Peter.

"A few years ago, new files began popping up. They weren't even hidden. At first it was new documents inside old folders. Then it was new files altogether. I recognized the Ripper connection and notified the Grandmaster. He called Andrews, and the result was our man Peter."

"And you don't know who's been adding the files?"

"No." Billingsworth shook his head. "Someone's violated procedure—someone who must think I'm a daft fool who can't keep proper track of my territory. It's bloody infuriating. I do my job, and I take violations seriously. I wanted to put a security system in, but then Andrews said the Brother would know that someone's been watching him. This way, we thought we could get to him without him knowing. It worked for my granddad."

"Your granddad was alive a hundred years ago. There is so much technology—" Charlie started.

"Yes, yes," Billingsworth retorted. "I'm aware of all the new gadgets that you young people play with. But I wonder if you are aware of the traditions. And as I said, it was not me who was against putting in security. It was that detective."

Billingsworth spit the word "detective" out as if he had just tasted some new, disgusting food which needed immediate regurgitation.

"Have you kept track of the new files?" Arden asked.

"I keep track of everything," Billingsworth said coolly.

"I didn't mean to insult you. I'm sorry. I just was wondering. Come to think of it, why wouldn't Andrews have you... Couldn't you guys put in cameras or something without telling the Brotherhood?"

"He said it would be too difficult. This is an old space. It's a strong space, but it's old. We installed a few new things; dehumidifier, the tube platform was built when the tube was built... But the problem is secrecy. This is a secret space. Barely anyone is privy to the actual location of the archives, and even fewer are allowed in. That's one reason for the code. The right code only allows for you to actually go into this space. Alec is not high enough in the Brotherhood to use it, but he received special permission from the Grandmaster last year."

"Why?"

"I wasn't told. They just told me to let him in. I assumed someone had his reasons. I have my own theories of course. I can't reveal them. It'd be against policy. It is strange, nevertheless. Lots of strange things have been going on. And as I said, the files have been coming... well I'd say for over five years. Alec wasn't even a Brother then."

"The tube platform. How... the tube is right there, I mean..."

"A Mason was on the planning committee. It was one of the first lines. You used to go out that way to get to the houses and such on London Bridge. It made for a convenient way for brothers to get in and out without revealing the location of the Lodge in the old days. With the burning down of the bridge, and the rebuilding, it became a little less important. The exit hadn't been used for years. However, when the tube was in the works, one of our senior Brothers recognized that we could have a quick route in and out without going through the Lodge tunnel if it passed right next-door. It isn't the only platform that has its own flag. There are other ones all over London."

"Like Down Street?"

"You've done your research in spades, young lady. Yes, like Down Street. But that one used to be a functioning tube stop. Now it's just a few feet of platform and a few abandoned rooms."

"What's Down Street?" Charlie asked.

"A tube stop that was abandoned because there are two other stops very close to it. It's between Hyde Park Corner and Green Park on the Piccadilly line. It wasn't destroyed, however, and it was used as secret war rooms by Churchill during World War II," Arden explained.

"Although this is a fascinating history lesson, we should be getting back to the subject at hand," suggested Billingsworth. "Is there anything that I can find for you two while we are having this little gathering?"

"Can I see the file that was out on the desk?" asked Peter.

Billingsworth retrieved the file and handed it to Peter.

"What about you two?" he asked Charlie and Arden.

"I'd like to see any files on Shakespeare," Arden said.

Charlie was still processing all the information given to him thus far. He stared at the jars along the wall. "What's in those?" he asked Billingsworth as he returned to the table.

"Ah yes. Well, the one that might interest you the most, young man, is this one."

Billingsworth took one of the cloudy and old jars off the shelf and put it on the table in front of Charlie.

"What is it?"

"Body parts. From the original Ripper victims. Stolen from their bodies on the streets of Whitechapel and preserved in these hallowed halls."

Arden stopped reading and stared at the jars. "You know, if you did DNA tests on those, you'd prove who the Ripper was!"

"Yes, but that will not happen, my dear. I think I've told you why. Not to mention the fact that you would first need DNA to compare." He put the jar back. "Have you found anything?"

Arden flipped through the file.

"No. There is nothing here that I didn't already know. What about you, Peter?"

"This has got all sorts of junk. Seems some of these blokes fancied themselves poets. Francis Thompson, J.K. Stephens... there's a whole lot of crap. They wrote some awful shite."

"Poets?" Charlie turned to Arden. "Like Shakespeare?"

"Yes, unfortunately young Thompson wasn't much good at anything. And to be frank, Stephens didn't amount to much, either. He did have some of his work published, but they are a bit rubbish, aren't they?" Billingsworth stopped talking and stared at a jar placed near the old Ripper victim jar.

"Well now, that's new."

"What?" Arden walked over and looked. Inside the jar was something that looked like a piece of intestine, some kidney, and a bit of liver. All from a human being. The jar was unlabeled, but she didn't need a label. She caught her breath as she realized that she was looking at the same body parts as in the old jar.

Billingsworth spoke first, "It seems our friend has left us pieces of the young ladies recently ripped. So to speak."

## Chapter 33

**"I have not kept my square, but that to come shall all be done by rule." - *Anthony and Cleopatra***

Alec paced back and forth. He had done everything that was asked of him. Now, he was just waiting for the next set of orders. He was growing impatient. His mind flitted back across time. It had been a year since he was inducted into the Brotherhood. The call had been surprising. He had no ties to the organization, and indeed had not actually known that much about them. When he got the call, he was not even told who had nominated him. Alec had always been an outsider, so he had been excited to be asked to be part of such an elite group. Apprentice Mason, he had thought. Wow, that sounded amazing. He learned quickly, and indeed, had risen quickly. His Benefactor's name had remained a mystery, but his status in the organization had demanded respect from circles that otherwise would not have acknowledged his existence. His Benefactor had been kind to him, letting him call and talk about nearly anything. Like a father, but one whom he would not recognize in a crowd. When Arden's dissertation became known to him, he first didn't pay much attention. He was listening to an interview she was conducting one day with Winston, when he realized what symbols she had been exploring. He became worried. He made the call to his Benefactor and expressed his concerns.

The Benefactor did not seem surprised. Rather, he seemed to not only expect this, but have a plan ready just in case. Then came Peter. Alec had not told his Benefactor about his friendship with Peter. Indeed, it didn't seem important. It was not until he had taken the book and given it to Peter that it was mentioned. His Benefactor had seemed calm, and only asked a few questions. Now, however, everything seemed to be tumbling out of control. Alec did not deal well with any loss of control, and indeed, was not handling this situation well at all.

The phone rang, forcing Alec out of his reverie. "Yes sir. No one else is here. I have an extra copy of it, but I don't understand.... Yes sir. I'll bring it there right now. Where is it, sir? Aldgate tube stop... by the old school... St. James' Passage. Yes, I'll find it... Yes. Thank you, sir." He hung up, grabbed a poster, and left for Mitre Square.

## Chapter 34

**"Our doubts are traitors, And make us lose the good we oft might win,**

**By fearing to attempt."-** ***Measure for Measure***

"That's evidence!" yelled Peter.

"It is that." Billingsworth sat down.

"I need to call Andrews. We need to do tests on this, mate!"

"It is against procedure to allow anything from the archives to leave the archives."

"But you didn't put it here!" Charlie insisted. "The parts in that jar aren't proper archives! Whoever put it here went against procedure, like you said!"

Billingsworth looked at Charlie. "Whoever put this here will know if it's gone."

They all thought about this for a minute.

"It must have been Alec! We know who put it here!"

"It could have been, but it could have been someone else. I don't know when it got here. I haven't been here since yesterday. I even missed the meeting earlier due to a prior engagement. Someone else could have brought it here."

"But it wasn't here yesterday?" Peter asked.

"That is certain. I would have seen it."

"That settles it." Peter picked up his phone. "Bugger all. No signal."

"We are fifty feet underground, my boy. Does that surprise you?"

"Sir," Arden said, "I respect your Brotherhood. I do not want to see it blamed for something for which it is not responsible. Please, let us take this to be tested. Even if a Brother put it here... If there are more murders... if the information that exists so far... three more women could be killed. This could be the only way to put a stop to it. As Charlie said, you spoke of people violating procedure. That's what is happening. Someone is desecrating your archives. This is the link. If the person who put this here comes looking for it... if we have it, we have a way of catching him. We need to find out the truth. Don't you see that?"

Billingsworth looked long and hard at Arden. He looked at Peter, and then at the jar. He sighed and closed his eyes. He was too old for this. The Americans were right. Too many had already died. This was larger than a jar in a room. This was hundreds of years of secrets... all jeopardized. He couldn't let that happen. He also couldn't let himself violate those oaths he had sworn to all those years ago. Billingsworth was an ardent Mason. He was also a practical man, and sometimes, although rules couldn't be broken, they might be bent a bit for the sake of the Brotherhood. He thought about his granddad. What would he do? What *had* he done? What would he have done if he had as much insight and technology as Billingsworth had?

This was not the first time the sacred archives had been violated, but by George, it would be the last. At least the last time on his watch.

After a few moments, Billingsworth opened his eyes and addressed his audience.

"I have an idea."

## Chapter 35

**"Love sought is good, but given unsought is better." - *Twelfth Night***

Arden and Charlie sat smashed into the driver's seat of the tube. They were on their way to Southwark. Again. It was getting late, and both were hungry. Once they were finally above ground, they headed straight for food so they could regroup. They had time. Peter was going to contact them when he needed them. It was after midnight, so pub food was out of the question. Their noses led them to a place that was open and sold kebabs. Arden hated kebabs, but she was so hungry she didn't care. It wasn't raining, so they got their food and headed to the boardwalk on the south bank of the Thames. They sat on a bench and ate in silence.

After some time, Charlie spoke. "Believe it or not," he said, "I've actually had a good time with you."

"Well no one ever accused me of being boring." Arden smiled. "Seriously, though, I'm glad you're with me."

"Me too." Charlie yawned.

"Tired?"

"Yeah."

"So am I. It has been a long day."

"You can say that again. Do you think we can go somewhere to get some sleep?"

"You can go back to your dorm if you want. I can get you when Peter calls. It could be hours."

"What, and leave you alone? Not on your life. There's some maniac out there killing innocent women."

Arden smiled. "Well, my apartment is right across from the Globe. Do you want to come over? You can crash on the couch."

"I'd like that." They shared a long look before getting up and walking over to Arden's apartment.

As they walked, Arden looked at Charlie and said, "Thank you for coming with me. I do feel better having you here. I never meant for you to have to deal with a full-fledged murder mystery. At least, not one that wasn't in a play."

"Don't worry, so do I. Feel better, I mean... what I'm trying to say is you don't have to thank me. I should be thanking you. I feel better being here. I've completely lost track of my depression. You've made me feel... This whole thing has just, well, made me feel... I guess that's it. Made me feel. Does that make any sense?"

Arden laughed, "Yes. It does. Sometimes that's all anyone needs. When bad things happen to me, I close up and just get numb. It helps, you know. Saves me the trouble of feeling bad. I don't feel anything. It's nice when you can finally pull out of that." She smiled. "Isn't it strange, how people always say things like 'you too'; even when a sales person says, 'enjoy the sweater', we always instantly respond, 'you too'—I'm rambling now. I'm sorry, Charlie."

"Don't be sorry. I like it when you ramble. I am always rambling. It's good that someone else does that, too."

Arden stopped and looked at Charlie. "I've only known you for two days. It seems like so much longer than two days."

They started walking again. After a few moments, Charlie replied, "Maybe it has been. I feel like we are in an alternate universe or something. A place where time moves... differently."

"I know what you mean."

"You know, Arden, if anyone was listening to us, they probably would think we were completely insane."

"Yep. Maybe we are. But if that's the case, I think I like insanity."

"So do I."

They arrived at Arden's apartment.

"Do you want any tea or anything?"

"Water actually would be great."

As Arden went to get water, Charlie looked around. The flat wasn't huge, but it was comfortable, and it smelled of roses; just like Arden. It had two bedrooms, one of which had been converted into a study. The living room area had a large red couch and two armchairs facing the TV. Behind them was a wide wall of windows that led to a balcony. The kitchen was to the right of the living room, and both bedrooms had doors that opened into the same main room. The one bathroom was between the two bedroom doors. Charlie looked around at the colorful posters: Star Wars, Salvador Dali, Andy Warhol, some Shakespeare... There was even a wall with posters from plays that Arden had worked on. She had made collages of various friends' faces, which seemed to be associated with the other posters. He peered into the bedrooms. Wow, he thought, there are posters everywhere. They gave a lived-in and homey feeling to the otherwise white walls. In fact, barely any wall space was visible. Any spot without a poster had massive bookcases. In the office, papers were piled everywhere. Charlie went back into the living room. He took the glass of water from Arden and went to sit down. As he did so, he noticed that in one corner was an enormous glass case full of colorful shapes. He got back up and walked over. The shapes materialized into their actual forms as he got closer. They were Star Wars toys. Lots and lots of Star Wars toys.

"I collect them," Arden admitted as Charlie stopped short in front of the cabinet.

"You are full of surprises, aren't you?"

"I try."

Charlie drank his water and placed the glass on the coffee table. He sat on the couch, letting his body sink into the red cushions. He hadn't noticed until now how tired he was. Within a minute, he was lying down, and within seconds he let himself descend into sleep.

Arden watched him as she puttered around the apartment. He looked so handsome lying peacefully on her sofa. She caught herself longing for him to wake up and come sleep in her bed with her. She looked away and headed into her room. She shouldn't feel this way, she thought. How old was he again? Twenty-two? Was that too young? She was twenty-eight, after all. That wasn't that many years. She had known him for such a short time and yet... It was almost too much to think about. Everything about him excited her. He didn't know her at all and yet, she felt like he knew her so well already. Every time he looked into her eyes she felt as if he was looking into her soul. Maybe it didn't matter... all the little things... his age... She lay down on her bed and let herself drift off into a world where there were no murder mysteries.

## Chapter 36

**"If circumstances lead me, I will find Where truth is hid, though it were hid indeed Within the centre." - *Hamlet***

Peter walked towards what used to be Berner Street, where the third Ripper victim had been found. A wave of fear swept over him as he looked around at the dimly lit buildings. It was in a place like this, he thought. His mind raced back to that night. Walking through the streets, searching for her with his younger brother clinging to his hand. Feeling them behind him, seeing the one holding his mother. Yelling without being able to make a noise. He tried. He tried to save her. He tried as hard as any five-year-old could have tried. By the time the police came, she was dead.

His decision to become a copper had so much to do with that horrible night. It was as if by solving other crimes, he would somehow find his own peace. It hadn't worked out like that, though. Each case was simply that: its own case. He had grown used to it. The detachment. It became routine, as did his dreams. Then he had been assigned to Arden.

Snap out of it, he said to himself. Focus on what you're doing. According to Arden, there had been a Working Men's Club next door to an alley, where Elizabeth Stride's body was found. He was quietly walking across the street towards the site when he saw a figure kneeling in the distance. It looked like a man bent over something. As he got closer he saw the man look up and shout:

"Lipski!"

Peter turned around to see what the kneeling man saw. A second man wearing a long elaborate cape came rushing towards him with a knife. Peter dodged so the man only cut the side of his arm. Peter recognized him immediately, despite the cape. It was Alec. He screamed at Peter who punched him with all of his strength. Alec fell backwards, and after managing to catch his balance, turned and ran towards a black car waiting at the end of the street. The other man had gotten up and had started running towards the car as well.

Peter, holding his arm, tried to run after them, but the car sped away. He turned and looked back at the site. There, right where Elizabeth Stride had been found, was a girl's body. He ran over and felt for a pulse. She was dead. He tugged out his mobile.

"Dammit" he heard himself say outloud. He picked up his phone and dialed. "Where are you buggers? I need help here!" he shouted.

He had called Andrews, and yelled into the phone, "They got 'er. Another one. She's dead. They cut me, too. Bastards! Get down here!"

He hung up and took out his badge as police started running out of the shadows. He showed his badge and yelled, "I'm a copper, you buggers! They went that way. Drivin' a black car. Headed towards the city!"

At this, all hell broke loose. Sirens atop marked cars with flashing lights emerged from everywhere. Peter hopped in one of the police cars and directed them towards old Mitre Square. He knew enough about the Ripper murders to know that if there was going to be another one tonight, it would be there. If the copycats were following the original as closely as they seemed to be, they would be headed there now. The murderers couldn't possibly get there too much before we do, he thought.

Andrews called Peter as he was racing to the next site. After filling Andrews in, Peter agreed to meet him at Mitre Square.

"We'll be ready for them," he muttered to himself.

When Peter and Andrews arrived at the site, things seemed eerily quiet. Mitre Square was similar to the way it had been a hundred years before. Police poured through every entryway into the square breaking the unnatural silence. Someone gave the signal, and ten police lights erupted at once. It was almost as bright as day. Peter let his eyes adjust to the light. He searched for the bench that faced St. James Passage. It had been moved about five feet forward from where it should have butted up against the short walls that held a grassy plot of land. Behind it, there was unmistakably a body.

Peter stared for a moment before he could speak. When he finally found his voice, the only thing that he could utter was, "Bollocks."

Andrews sighed in agreement. "We are too late."

## Chapter 37

**"But screw your courage to the sticking place." - *Macbeth***

A few hours later, a loud ringing woke Charlie. He crept into Arden's room. "Arden. Arden, wake up... do you hear that?"

"Huh? Hear what? Charlie? What's going on?" she said sleepily. Then she heard the ringing. She got up instantly and grabbed her phone.

"Hello? Who is it?"

"Blimey, it's me, who d'you think it is?" Arden sighed as she recognized Peter's voice.

"I'm sorry, we must have fallen asleep."

"Never mind that. Get up and get down here. A car will be there for you in about five minutes." With that, the line went dead.

"Charlie? We are being picked up and taken somewhere. Something's happened." She blearily turned on the lights. Then she went into the living room where Charlie was throwing on his coat. The buzzer sounded from downstairs. Arden grabbed her jacket, umbrella, and purse, and the two headed out into the cold and foggy air to meet the car.

When they got to Mitre Square, a bloodstained Peter greeted them.

"Oh, my God. Peter, are you all right?" Arden shivered.

"I'm fine, luv. Dandy. It's just me arm. I'm a bleeder, but I'll be all right. Surface wound. Already bandaged and everythink."

Peter's arm had bled all over, but the cut was not that deep. The thick bandage the paramedics put on made it look worse than it was.

"What happened? Where's Andrews?"

"What d'you think happened, luv? He's around here somewhere."

"What happened to you?" asked Charlie.

"Well, I found our friend. He wasn't the one who cut me, though. That was Alec."

"Alec?"

"I went to the site of the third killing, and sure enough, there was a man leaning over somethink on the ground. He shouts this word at me, Liski or somethink..."

"Lipski? asked Arden.

"Yeah, that's the one. Then, who d'ya think came out of bloomin' nowhere! Alec. He's holdin' a knife. He says somethink like, 'Peter, you need to stop being where you shouldn't.' Can you imagine? I slug him one when he cuts me and runs off, coward that he is. I look back and the bastard's gone. I went over to the girl who's been ripped good and dead. That's when I called Andrews. All the coppers started comin', so I told Andrews I was comin' 'ere."

"Do you know who the girl was?"

"Nope. My guess is another actress, ya know, one playing one of the witches, but they were wearin' so much make up for the show that I couldn't tell, yeah? Andrews 'as got men out on the streets lookin' for Alec and the other bloke. We got here 'spectin' to find 'em, and look, they got the other one already."

Peter led Charlie and Arden to the side of the square where a sheet already covered the body.

"Too little time has passed," said Arden after a moment, shivering.

"What do you mean?" asked Charlie.

"These two Ripper murders happened in the same night. But less than 24 hours separated the first two, which was wrong. Many days separated the original ones. I wonder if there are two in one night..."

"How did he find them?" asked Charlie. "And how did he get them here?"

"They're easy 'nough t' find," said Peter. "Havin' a memorial service at the rehearsal hall."

"He found them and brought them to these sites." Andrews seemed to come out of nowhere. "You will not be surprised to know that both murdered women were part of the *Macbeth* cast. The strange thing seems to be that the one Peter happened upon was the second to die, although according to the order of the original murders, she should have been the first. She only had her throat cut, whereas this one was mutilated. Sound familiar? Not only that, but it seems the 'Long Liz' victim was drugged in addition to having her throat cut. It's bloody cold out here, British weather at its best. Cold nights even in summer. I think we all need a cup of tea."

They all headed to a nearby inn where the police had set up shop. Andrews ordered someone to put the kettle on.

"Mutilated?" asked Charlie.

"Yep," Arden responded. "When Catherine Eddowes was found, her body was on its back, the head turned to the left. The right leg bent at the knee, the palms open. Her abdomen was exposed and most of her intestines were placed over her right shoulder. About two feet of her intestines were cut out and placed between her body and her left arm. Her throat had been cut, as were her nose, ear, and jaw. Her left kidney was taken out, along with part of her uterus. The liver had been badly cut up. You should see the mortuary photo at some point. It's awful. The physician who examined the body said that it would definitely have to be someone with medical or anatomical knowledge who killed her because he thought the kidneys would be hard to find."

"Thank you, my dear; now we don't have to wait for the coroner's report," Andrews grunted. "And, there goes the double event," he continued. "I called Edward. He is beside himself, naturally. Alec is nowhere to be found, and my men are coming up empty."

"You said the man bent over the body shouted 'Lipski'?" Arden asked Peter, ignoring Andrews' comments.

"Yup. Don't know why, though."

"Oh, and do you mind clearing up the double event thing?" Charlie asked.

Arden looked at Charlie first. "The night Elizabeth Stride, otherwise known as Long Liz, and Catherine Eddowes were killed is known as the double event because both were killed in that same night. Liz Stride only had her throat cut, as if the man didn't have time to finish, which brings us to the Lipski comment."

She turned to Peter. "When Long Liz was murdered, a man was crossing on the other side of the street. His name was Israel Schwartz. He saw two men. One seemed to be holding a woman on the ground. The crouched man shouted the word *lipski* at him. That's when Schwartz noticed the other man, who seemed to be coming after him. Schwartz ran, and didn't stop until he was a safe distance away and sure he wasn't followed. That word was used regularly at the time. There had been a Jewish man named Lipski who had been on trial for killing his wife. The word became a negative term for Jews."

Charlie caught up with Arden. "So, because the guys who committed these murders knew about the right order of the Ripper murders, they would know that as soon as someone found the Liz girl, they'd go looking for the other girl. If they wanted to completely re-enact the killing, they would need to wait for someone to come by so they could shout that word at them."

"Exactly—" Arden began.

Charlie's excitement intensified. "What if the girl was drugged and maybe the killers were waiting for you to get there?" He looked at Arden, and continued, "You or

Peter, or me, anyone for that matter. If they were re-enacting the crime, they might have waited for all the parts to be in place!"

"Good point," said Andrews. "But how would they have known Peter would come by?"

"It probably could have been anyone. Since there are police out monitoring the scenes of the original crime, they would expect someone to show up."

"What is really strange, though," Arden pointed out, "is the fact that this Mitre Square murder had already happened when you got here."

"That's easy 'nough, luv," Peter said, "Like the lad said, the bastard'd know we'd come here after findin' the first one. He thought he'd beat us to it by doin' the first, second."

"I suppose," Arden said. "Something isn't making any sense."

"It's beginning to, though. At least, I think it is starting to come together," Charlie said to Arden.

Andrews looked at him quizzically. "I'm glad you think so. I, on the other hand, could not agree less."

Charlie's eyes did not move from Arden's.

Andrews sighed, "Well, I do hope the Billingsworth chap is right and this plan of yours works. Otherwise we are going to find some unfortunate young lady in pieces in the not-too-distant future. We now only have the Mary Kelly murder to look forward to."

"Are they going to shut down the show?" asked Charlie.

"The show? Oh, with two more actresses dead, you mean. That's for Edward to say. I wouldn't think so, although it would be a grand idea."

"How did the girl get here? I mean, they couldn't have both just happened to have been at the proper spots to copy Jack the Ripper," commented Charlie.

"Another mystery. Yes. They were both found where the first victims were; exactly where we expected to find them." Andrews shook his head. "This won't stay out of the papers now. It's almost daybreak. My men will not be able to hide this."

Arden interrupted, "Peter, you said they were having a memorial service. And then, as Charlie pointed out, one at least was probably drugged. What if the killer showed up at the service, and took the two girls out with him, drugged them, and then brought them to the respective sites? Someone must have noticed them leave the service. Someone there must have seen the man or men who led them away."

"Yes, but we know Alec has something to do with this, and he was probably the one who took them out of the service. He was a member of the Globe staff, and would have been welcome at such a gathering," Andrews pointed out.

Charlie snapped out of his trance. "That message, the one you were talking about, Arden... Was it written anywhere?"

Arden smiled at Charlie. "You remembered. I didn't even remember."

"What message exactly? And is there more tea ready?" Andrews bellowed to the server.

Arden explained about the Juwes message as they received their refills. Andrews chugged his tea and then placed a call to one of the officers back at the station. A few minutes later, the call came back. There was indeed a message written in chalk on a nearby wall.

The four headed back out into the cold fog and over to the side wall of the nearby street.

"'The Juwes are the ones who will be blamed for nothing,'" Andrews read.

"But that's not it." Arden frowned. "I mean, it's close, but the message originally read 'will *not* be blamed for nothing.' Is someone taking a picture this time?"

"Yes, my dear, this is not Victorian London. We not only have cameras, we also document all evidence," he snapped.

Peter looked at Arden. "What the devil are you talkin' 'bout, the wrong message? What in the hell does that mean? Will be blamed, will not be blamed?"

"When the message was copied down, one person wrote 'will be blamed' as opposed to 'will not be blamed.' The 'will not be' is generally agreed upon as being correct. In choosing to get rid of the word 'not', the killer must be making some sort of point," Arden explained.

Andrews was speaking to someone on his mobile. "We are taking DNA samples from everything, in the spirit of modern technology. Including your arm, Peter. Take off your jacket. It needs to be bagged as evidence. Another testament to modern versus Victorian London. I'll be damned if the Ripper gets away twice."

Despite the cold that descended on the city and the late hour, a crowd was forming around Mitre Square. The police had sectioned off the area, but there were still many people who had appeared to find out the cause of the large police presence. Arden walked towards the body, looking for something, although she didn't quite know what, when she saw a familiar face in the crowd. It was Hendry. He was yelling something at one of the officers. Andrews approached Hendry and demanded to know what he wanted. Arden moved closer so she could hear.

"I am the head of an educational organization which holds close ties to the Globe Theatre. You have one of my educators with you now, in fact. I am merely eager to know whether it is safe for her and her student to remain in their field of study. I need to know what is going on at once."

"Richard, what are you doing here?" Arden asked.

Hendry seemed taken aback to see Arden actually standing on the other side of the police line. When he noticed Charlie standing next to her, he became livid. "Dr. James. I demand that you and your student leave this area immediately. You are putting your life and the life of your student in jeopardy, as well as the integrity of this institution. You will come with me."

"I'm sorry, Richard," Arden said. "That is not possible."

Hendry turned a shade of red that Charlie had never seen in nature.

Andrews replied to Hendry's demands in a tone of voice that dictated the finality of the argument. "Arden James and Charlie Leder have been a tremendous help to Scotland Yard's investigation. We will not permit her to leave this scene until I feel it is necessary. At that time, she is to resume her research into this case. You, sir, have no authority here. You may leave."

Arden turned away and returned to the body. Andrews headed towards the wall. Charlie stayed in place, staring at Hendry as he angrily made his way out of the crowd.

"Huh," Charlie said, and then to no one in particular, "am I the only one who doesn't understand why he's been at the scene of the last two crimes?"

"No. I was wondering about that, too." Arden came up behind him.

"You shouldn't sneak up on people at murder scenes."

"I'm sorry. I just was worried. But I agree with you. Why was he here? How did he even know to come here?"

"Arden!" shouted Andrews. "You want to have a look at this."

They walked back towards the wall. The writing was on something white, not on the wall itself, but on something taped to the wall, backwards. The detective removed it and turned it over. There, with the threatening message on the back, was a copy of the same *Tempest* poster that had hung in Winston's office. Andrews shined his flashlight on the ground below where the poster had been. According to Police Reports, there had been a piece of Catherine Eddowes' apron lying at the site. Here, instead of an apron, there was a bloody pile of paper, which, when she looked closer, Arden recognized at once. It was yet another copy of her dissertation.

Before anyone could react, a loud scream pierced through the crowd.

"Oh, my sweet Jesus! Look at this, y'all! A real British crime scene! Isn't this just the best!"

"Oh, no. It's not..." Charlie whispered.

"How did she get here? How did she—?" Before Arden could finish, Mary Jo's screeching drawl continued, increasing in volume with every word.

"Charlie! I thought that was you! And Dr. James, right? I am just so excited! We had the TV on in the common room, and this newsman said there'd been a murder, and well, we just had to come look! Isn't this just the most wild thing? Hey, how come y'all get to be on the cool side of the rope? Will y'all let me in? I brought my camera!"

The look that Andrews gave Mary Jo could have killed the Globe actress if she wasn't already dead.

"Dr. James, do we know this person?" Andrews queried stonily.

The police line that Mary Jo was standing behind was just close enough to the group that she was able to react before Arden could find her voice.

"Are you a real British detective? Oh my God. This is just plum wonderful! Wait until my friends back home hear about this. Can I see the body? I just love mysteries! That Nancy Drew, now some say that she's just an old fuddy duddy and they like some of those newer mysteries better, but I say; go with the old."

"You know, Mary Jo, um, I heard that... there was... the Queen is going to be coming to take a look," Charlie stammered.

"Are you serious!" she squealed at the top of her lungs. "The real queen? I just love her!"

Arden took her cue from Charlie. "Yeah, ah, um, we need someone to be on the lookout. You know, in case she comes. Do you mind, uh, going over to that main highway back there? Near the Aldgate tube stop? You can run over and tell us when she gets here."

"Oh my God! Do you mean it? Little old me? Are you sure! Although, that William, now, he is just the cutest thing ever! Well, not as cute as my boyfriend Johnny Red, but he's awful close."

"I heard he's coming with her," Charlie said hurriedly.

"Are you serious? How do I look? Oh, my face is probably as messy as half-eaten pie! How could I possibly show myself? What would I say?"

"You look lovely, my dear girl. Why don't you think about your greeting to the prince as you walk away from here?" Andrews was fuming, but if this was the only way to get this damned girl away from his murder scene, he'd go along with it. Mary Jo's voice was still echoing through Mitre Square as Andrews' deputy led her away from the scene towards Aldgate Street.

"I think that is enough interruption for one day." With that, Andrews led the group over to his police car, and back to Scotland Yard.

## Chapter 38

**"Good things of day begin to droop and drowse; While night's black agents to their preys do rouse." - *Macbeth***

The Benefactor sat in front of a fireplace mulling things over. This had not gone according to plan. Peter was not supposed to get hurt. He was supposed to die. He had seen too much, knew too much. Luckily, he wasn't bright enough to put the pieces together, but Arden was. With her poking about, everything was getting a bit too dangerous.

*However, I thrive on danger,* thought the Benefactor. *It's just a matter of picking up where I left off. Synthesizing all the new information. With Arden becoming a larger part of the investigation, the whole operation would have to take on a faster, not to mention more intense tone.*

"Bloody Americans."

He sighed and stared at the fire. It was time to focus. *The greatest thinkers had to overcome obstacles,* he thought. The Brotherhood stood because of hundreds of years of overcoming adversity.

"This might just work in our favor," the Benefactor said to himself. An idea was beginning to form. It would be risky, of course, but in truth, what wasn't? The problem from the start had been the final victim. Arden was bright, to be sure, but far too nosey. And it was her book that had given them their cue. From the start, that problem needed to be eliminated. There would be too many questions and no one to answer them.

"Yes. That will work."

The Benefactor smiled to himself as he went back over the night's events in his mind. There had been minor snags, of course, but all in all, things did not go badly. He opened the metal box that sat next to him. Here, too, he could not proceed exactly as history would have dictated. However, he would be close enough. More than one hundred years ago, George Lusk, the chairman of the Vigilance Committee, received a cardboard box wrapped in brown paper. It contained part of a kidney soaked in wine. It also contained a letter indicating the sender had eaten the other half of the kidney. After much deliberation and discussion, the majority agreed that the kidney was indeed from Catherine Eddowes. Of course, without the technology, Scotland Yard would never know for sure, and the debate would continue into the next millennium.

This half could not be sent to just anyone. Of course, the other half was to be put with the others, but this half... He looked at the kidney in the metal box. Ahh, he thought. Regardless of any American interference, I am still one step ahead. Those idiots. Always looking in the wrong direction.

With that, he picked up the phone and made a call. "Did Alec go over there?"

The voice at the other end replied, "Yes."

"Good. Call him and tell him to stay there. Instruct him I shall be over later today to congratulate him, and tell him to make himself comfortable."

## Chapter 39

**"God has given you one face and you make yourselves another." - *Hamlet***

Andrews glared at Arden and Charlie during most of the drive. Arden could not contain her embarrassment. No wonder. How can anyone be so clueless, she thought? Charlie was even more humiliated. Mary Jo was the reason that all these people approached him as if he were the devil. Ugh. Both of them silently agreed to pretend that nothing happened. No one mentioned Mary Jo again. The whole group had moved back to the police station where Andrews demanded his seventh cup of tea. With the exception of ten minutes, during which he had traveled from the pub to Scotland Yard, and another three dedicated to phone calls, Andrews had continued an alternating pattern of pacing and drinking tea. He had become remarkably quiet. Arden was telling the others about Catherine Eddowes' history of drunkenness when Andrews finally burst into the conversation.

"This is bollocks. Tell me, young lady, what should I know that I don't already? There have been four murders. That's done. Bollocks to them. There's one left. Who was she again?"

"Mary Jane Kelly," Arden replied with exaggerated slowness, irritated. She felt as if she had repeated herself fifty times so far. For someone who had the original police documents sitting in his office, Andrews seemed remarkably ignorant. Charlie sat down next to Arden. He was leaning on his arm so that his head was tilted towards her. She realized that she could just barely feel his long curls touching her cheek. She let herself acknowledge how incredibly soft his hair was. It was so curly; she didn't expect it to be so soft. She had been answering one question after another, but they seemed to hit a wall with the investigation. Her dissertation had been found underneath the girl who had been the second one murdered that night, the Long Liz victim. She was the first one Peter found, and the first one according to Ripper history. However, the order was decidedly altered tonight for what was most likely convenience's sake. Not much else had been decided or agreed upon.

Andrews' voice snapped her back to life.

"Right, now, Arden. Tell me, isn't there a theory that says Mary Kelly is the most important victim?"

Arden sighed. "There are a few. There's one that is the most well known, and in which the Masons are very important. It's the royal conspiracy theory. It says Prince Eddy was apprentice to the painter Walter Sickert. Mary Kelly was the focus point because it was alleged that she was spreading information or attempting to blackmail the Prince. She had allegedly witnessed a secret Catholic marriage between Prince Eddy and the prostitute, Annie Crook, which resulted in the birth of a legitimate child. It's Stephen Knight's theory. In fact, Catherine Eddowes is considered by Stephen Knight to be a mistake because she often went by the name Mary Kelly. See, she was seeing a man named John Kelly, and the name Mary was so common, she used it as a decoy for when she was in any trouble with the law. In fact, the night of the murder she had been in jail and had used that name. She was killed shortly after she was released. In an attempt to find a pattern to the locations, Knight and others have discounted the final location because they look at the Eddowes' murder as the last intended killing. It was only when the murderers realized they had made a mistake that they went to Millers Court and murdered the real Kelly. Knight claims that by taking the first four murder points and drawing lines between them, you get a pentacle square. Other Ripperologists claim that the four points point an arrow to Parliament—indicating high-up conspiracy."

"I remember the theory about the Prince's marriage to a prostitute in a Catholic church and the birth of a legitimate baby," acknowledged Andrews.

Arden nodded. "According to Knight, Mary Kelly was also an object of affection to the painter, Walter Sickert. He allegedly used her likeness in his later works. At the time, Knight claimed that she involved her friends in an attempt at blackmail, which is when the Ripper started first dispatching her friends and then finally herself."

"And Sickert was the one who allegedly introduced the prince to Annie Crook?"

"Yes. There are other Mary Kelly theories, though. In another theory, it was her lover who committed the murders because he didn't want her to be a prostitute. He committed the first four to scare her, but when that didn't work, he brutally killed her."

"But that theory doesn't have to do with the Masons."

"No. It is irrelevant to us. I mean, we are definitely dealing with something that has Masonic connections, and if a Mason was involved, back then or today, Mary Kelly would be the object of interest. It simply goes along with the conspiracy theory, which is not altogether accurate in most opinions, including mine, but it is one of the more widely known theories thanks to several films."

He thought for a moment. "Arden, I do not want you to stay in your apartment for a while. Is there someplace that you can go?"

"What do you mean? Why?"

Andrews sighed. "I have a feeling that you might be more involved than you think."

"What do you mean?" asked Charlie.

"Arden, you are bright enough to put this together, I'm sure. You know that in all these new cases, copies of your omniscient dissertation were at the scenes."

"This guy must have spent a fortune at Kinko's," Charlie joked.

Arden was the only one who laughed. "Charlie, they don't have Kinko's here."

"Oh."

Andrews gave Charlie a look that could have killed a rat.

"Listen to me, my dear," he said sternly, turning to Arden. "You are following this investigation. Your dissertation was at the crime scenes. Someone wants you to be traipsing about Whitechapel looking for clues. You are the knowledgeable person in this case. You are the one with the confidential information. Don't you understand? You are a target. The murderer has made you a target."

Charlie thought for a minute. "You think that Arden is their Mary Kelly?" Charlie instantly sat beside her, protective and close.

"It seems to be a strong possibility at the very least." Andrews poured himself another cup of tea and loaded it with sugar.

They sat in silence for a minute. Finally, she spoke. "The last one will be hard. Mary Kelly was killed in her room. A room that doesn't exist anymore. Millers Court is now a parking garage across from White's Row."

"That may be true, but it doesn't change the fact that—"

"I know," interrupted Arden. "And if we don't find these guys soon, you might be right. I, for one, know we're getting close. We are so close that it doesn't make sense to stop now."

Andrews opened his mouth to object, but Arden stopped him.

"Look, I won't be alone, okay? I won't leave Charlie's side, and if I am targeted, then use me as bait. I'm not going to hide out like a scared bunny. If I know too much, let's use it to our advantage. We are just too close."

## Chapter 40

**"The art of our necessities is strange, That can make vile things precious." - *King Lear***

The Benefactor sat staring at all the files. It always amazed him how well the records had been kept. There were so many hundreds of years of history that existed in this one room. He thought about the first time he had been privy to the secret hallway. It was Good Friday, but he had left church early to attend a meeting. Considering how observant he was, it had been a huge sacrifice. He hoped that the meeting would be finished in enough time for him to attend the midnight mass. In addition, he was exhausted from the disciplines. He fasted that Friday, as he had every Friday. Even so, he did not think that abstaining from meat was enough penitence. Christ died for our sins, after all.

Knowing how religious he was, the Brothers had chosen that particular day for a reason. They were dissuaded from discussing religion, as the only commonly held religious bond was the belief in God. It had been that way since the Pope had turned on the Knights so many years ago. However, many of the Brothers were friends, and they knew the depth of his beliefs.

It turned out, to his surprise, to be his initiation ceremony. He was to become a Master Mason on Good Friday. It almost gave him chills just thinking about it. The ceremony would become routine in time, but that day, it was amazing. He had been blindfolded, and the Porter ushered him inside. He had no idea what he was experiencing, and it was only at the end that he was told about the allegory.

The recreation of the deaths of Hiram Abiff and his murderers was terrifying. He was forced to play the part of the fated Temple of Solomon architect while each of the three 'Juwes' performed their ritualistic 'killing' on him. The brothers led him through the re-enactment. He had been blindfolded. First, Jubella had asked for the secrets of the master. He refused, and a four-inch gauge had slipped across his throat. The second, Jubello, asked the same question. The result had been a strike on the chest by a square. The third, Jubellum, asked as well, was refused again, and he was dealt a blow on the head. He finally was dragged down to the floor as if dead and the Brothers left him, going off in 'search' of the master architect.

The three are heard condemning themselves with the well-known punishments, which would become the Masonic oaths:

The first said, "Oh that my throat be cut across, my tongue torn out by the roots, and my body buried in the sea."

The second responded, "Oh that my breast be torn open, my heart and vitals taken from thence and thrown over my left shoulder."

The third echoed through the others. "Oh that my body be severed in twain, my bowels taken from thence and burned to ashes."

The punishments had been 'given' by the Juwe, and his body 'found' when the Grandmaster took his hand and raised him up. They had assumed the position, hand to back, foot to foot, knee to knee, breast to breast, mouth to ear: the five points of fellowship.

When it was all over, the Grandmaster spoke the unforgettable words, "Let the Brother see the Light." The blindfold came off to reveal the chamber, beautiful in the elaborate maze of candlelight.

That day he pledged his whole heart and soul to the Brotherhood knowing that it was a sign from above that Good Friday, the day his Savior had died for the sins of all, he should be put through the re-enactment of death. He too had been resurrected. The Benefactor closed his eyes, feeling the full weight of his pride.

A noise from the passage forced him back to the present. Alec would be here shortly. What a pity, he thought. Such a nice lad. So kind and devoted to the Brotherhood. He would have made a wonderful Master. However, sloppiness could not go unpunished. Sloppiness caused trouble for the Brotherhood, and that could not be tolerated. He had introduced Peter to them. Peter was supposed to die by Alec's hand. It was part of the plan. True, it had not been part of the original killings, but some things had to be amended to suit the times. Peter had betrayed them. He had attended secret meetings under a false pretense. This could not be allowed to continue. In addition, there was no doubt that every police officer in London would be looking for Alec now, and the Benefactor could not risk the connection.

Alec had never met him. At least not face to face in his true form. He knew the lad would be as giddy as a schoolboy and eager for his reward. The Benefactor sighed with all the weight of regret.

True to form, Alec entered the room in a deeply respectful and penitent manner and stared at the hooded man who sat erect at the table. Shadows from the sparse assortment of candles made it impossible to divine any features beneath the protection of the hood.

"Sir? I thank you for granting me the opportunity to serve the Brotherhood. I am sorry to have failed in the full fulfillment of my task."

"It's all right, my son," came the voice from the cloak. "I know your heart was in the right place."

"I promise I will not fail again. He will die."

"There is no need to make such a promise. You will not be trying to correct your mistake. You must be content with my forgiveness and make peace with your sins."

Alec was confused, but grateful. He had thought of Peter as a friend and could not believe that such a friend would betray the Brotherhood. "Thank you, sir. If you don't mind me asking, what should I do then?"

The figure rose from the table and walked over to Alec. The cloak covered every part of his body. Alec struggled to see his face, but the hood came down too far.

The cloaked man put his arm on Alec's shoulder as if to comfort him.

"Just be at peace, my son."

The knife plunged deep into Alec's body. Shocked, Alec grabbed at the wound, and slipped to the ground, catching sight of the face beneath the hood as he fell.

"It's... it's you..." The true identity of his Benefactor froze on his lips as he issued his last breath.

## Chapter 41

**"And as imagination bodies forth, The forms of things unknown,**

**the poet's pen, Turns them to shapes and gives to airy nothing, A local habitation and a name." - *A Midsummer Night's Dream***

Arden tossed and turned in Charlie's bed.

"Why did I let them talk me into this?" she asked herself. "If they look for me at my flat and I'm not there, won't this be the next place they'll look?"

Her arguments had been in vain. There were two places she was not to go. One was her flat and the other was The George. That made even less sense, but Peter insisted that both were places she was known to frequent, and therefore obvious places to look for her. Why was Peter being so adamant? She hadn't understood him. Surely, he didn't care that much about her. What sleep would she get anyway? They had just seen one of the grisliest murders. They had only been allowed a moment's glance at the girl's body, cut up in the exact same manner as the body of Catherine Eddowes. Arden had looked away quickly, but the picture stayed pasted in her mind. She shouldn't have looked. She knew what was there, but curiosity had gotten the better of her.

Arden turned over in vain. It had been after 5 A.M. when they got back to Charlie's anyway, and now it was after six and beginning to become light outside. Why bother trying to sleep? She wasn't comfortable, and it wouldn't be too long before she would have to get up. She turned over and noticed Charlie shivering in the chair where he was trying to sleep.

"Come here and share the bed," she insisted.

He weighed his options for a moment. "Are you sure? It's not a big bed."

"No, that's for sure. It's one of the smallest twin beds in the world, but I don't mind. Come on, get in. I promise to only bite if you want me to."

He laughed, "Ok, thanks".

"Besides," she said, "I have the warm blanket and you're freezing. We'll cuddle. Here."

She sat up and shifted over, picking up the blanket and laying it on top of him once he climbed in. He edged himself in and, in no time, she felt the weight of Charlie's body pressing against hers.

"Comfy?" he said.

"Yes, actually. You?"

"Surprisingly, yes. You are a comfortable pillow."

She laughed, feeling herself lapse into teenager mode. She loved the feeling of his body near hers.

"I don't know how much sleep we can get anyway. It's beginning to get light outside," she said.

"So we won't sleep. We'll just lay here and talk about happy things. What's your favorite color?"

"That's an odd question. I would have to say purple."

"I thought so."

He wedged himself so he was staring deeply into her eyes.

"You look like a purple person."

"What exactly does a purple person look like?"

"Well," he said, shifting so they were sharing the pillow. Their bodies seemed attached from the shoulder down. "A purple person is artistic, creative, and often finds themselves in crazy situations, like hundred-year-old murder mysteries. I myself am a blue person. Sympathetic to the purple cause, of course, but not so adept at handling it."

"I would say that fits. You look like a blue person. I wonder what green or red people look like? Probably just like me, but a bit less shady?"

Charlie took a deep breath. She smelled so much like roses. It was comforting. He was quiet for a moment before speaking.

"You look beautiful," he finally said.

For a moment, time stood still, and all of the craziness went away. She leaned over and kissed him. The world around her disappeared, and Arden felt nothing but peace. It was the most perfect kiss in the world.

Charlie smiled and kissed her back, passionately.

Arden's own passion rose, and her hands sought his clothes under the duvet.

At 7am, sweaty, exhausted and content, the ringing of Charlie's phone interrupted the beauty of the moment. Reluctantly, Charlie pulled away and answered it.

"Hello? Oh. Hi, Mom. Yes, I'm fine. I know you told me to call you daily, but... all right, all right. Yes, everything's good. Mom, it's the middle of the night, can I... Yes, I promise I will call you later. Thanks, I know... tell Dad I say hi. Yes. You, too. Bye, Mom."

Charlie hung up, turning red from embarrassment.

"Well, now you look like a red person."

"I'm sorry about that."

"We all have parents. I know how it is. They tend to worry about you."

Charlie looked at Arden's smiling face. He relaxed again and pulled her back into a kiss. After a minute, another phone rang. This time it was Arden's mobile.

"Damn! What is up with this? It's probably *my* mother."

"Then we'd be even," Charlie snickered.

She reached around and took her phone from her bag.

"Hello?"

"Arden?" came Andrews' gruff voice. "You have to get down here immediately."

"Get down where?"

"To the Globe. Now."

She hung up the phone.

"Not your mom, I take it."

"Nope, Andrews."

"What happened? Have we been called back to duty?" Charlie murmured his face in her hair.

"Yeah, Andrews has great timing, huh?"

"Perfect. Have I ever told you how much I don't like that man?"

Arden giggled. "I agree. But we had better go. He sounded frantic."

"He always sounds frantic."

"Yup. It seems we've been summoned to the Globe Theatre."

"Of course," sighed Charlie. "Everyone gets summoned to the Globe Theatre at 7 in the morning."

With that they got out of bed, and left Bankside to report to duty.

**Chapter 42**

**"We have seen better days." - *Timon of Athens***

At the Globe, things were in a state of chaos. The rain had started up again, forcing a barrage of officers onto the covered stage and into the backstage rooms. Andrews was yelling orders at officers while trying to calm down a crazed Edward Filbin. The two things were not happening in a harmonious fashion. Arden and Charlie were ushered to the back wall of the stage where Andrews had set up camp. As soon as he saw them, he stopped talking to Edward and started shouting at them.

"All the *Tempest* posters are gone. There is not a single one anywhere. ANYWHERE! Do you understand me? What the devil does the bloody *Tempest* have to do with Jack the Ripper? You are the expert! Tell me now!"

Of course, as he was shouting this, Edward was shouting his own frustrations at the new entrants. "I'm short TWO witches AND a porter. HOW AM I SUPPOSED TO WORK?! WHO THE DEVIL IS DOING THIS?! This is insane. And you two just RUNNING off the way you did today. How can you POSSIBLY understand, or DO you possibly understand that the WHOLE future of the Globe, let alone my CAREER, is at stake?"

As Arden attempted to filter both commands, or questions rather, a voice broke through the madness.

"QUIET! BOTH OF YOU!" Charlie had stood on a chair and grabbed a megaphone. Still speaking through it, he shouted, "HOW CAN YOU POSSIBLY EXPECT HER TO ANSWER ANYTHING WHILE YOU ARE BOTH SHOUTING AT THE SAME TIME?"

They were both silent, and all eyes were on Arden. Nervously, she began. "Well, to start, I'm very sorry about your cast, Edward. I don't know what to say except I suggest you close for a day or two to regroup. It will cost money, but it might also give us the time we need to clean up this mess."

Edward started to interrupt, but Arden stopped him. "I am a director, as well, and I know that is the last thing you want to do, but considering the body count, you do not have much choice. Detective Andrews, the connection between the Ripper and the *Tempest* is simple once you notice it. The Elizabethan mystic, John Dee, was a noted Rosicrucian. The *Tempest* is said to have been about him and incorporates several Rosicrucian concepts. In addition, the Globe itself is built on the principles of Sacred Geometry according to the Knights. This is significant because whomever we are dealing with is going out of his way to show his connection to the Knights. The connections are endless.

"In my dissertation, I speak about this movement in depth, and go into great detail about how symbolism in the *Tempest* is one of the strongest connections we have when linking Shakespeare to this order. Even Prospero, the main character in the Tempest, is named for one who gives joy and prosperity by enabling others to prosper which is the mark of a true master mason. Prospero describes himself as "Prospero the prime, reputed in dignity and for the Liberal Arts without a parallel... having both the key of officer and office... all dedicated to closeness". I maintain that the *Tempest* is not only a tribute to John Dee, but also the way that Shakespeare was able to express his love for the Brotherhood as a whole. It would have been performed at the Globe, and it was one of the last plays Shakespeare wrote. By focusing the play on the occult and science, he incorporates both of Dee's primary interests, while staying away from strong religious elements.

"The Brotherhood, as I have said before, is not and has never been religious. It would, however, have been a place that encouraged religious freedom. This provided the members a sort of protection at the time, as it was only a few years away from the Puritan Revolution, and not too far removed from Bloody Mary or Mary Queen of Scots—both Catholic martyrs. Hence, this is a time where religion was deathly important, so to speak. Queen Elizabeth and King James worked to unite the country under the Church of England, killing the occasional dissenter or fanatic on charges of treason.

"The question remains: is this Ripper a Mason? Keeping in mind that we are not attempting to find out about the original Ripper, I still believe he was not a Brother. However, this case is different, and using these symbols shows that this Ripper *is* a Brother. By using the *Tempest* poster to write his message, he is underlining a connection with the Masons. Therefore, this Ripper is probably part of the Brotherhood and wants to make some sort statement. He is obviously offended that I reveal so many Masonic symbols in Shakespeare, which are probably considered private knowledge, or possibly even sacred references. All I was trying to do was link different symbols in Shakespeare, but that is not the way this guy is taking it. He purposely is choosing symbols, which I have pointed out, and purposely using the Ripper murders, something that has murmurs of

Masonic conspiracy, to make his point—whatever his point is. I have a feeling that whenever we figure that part out, we will have solved the mystery."

Silence filled the space. After a few minutes, Charlie's voice replaced the void. "What this boils down to really is the link between Shakespeare and the Ripper: that Shakespeare probably was a Mason, and that there is a theory that a Mason was the Ripper. That's it. That's the only thing."

"Yes. That's it. There is no other connection. I mean, I suppose it is possible that the original Ripper was also an actor. Maybe he was an actor who performed the role of Prospero in the *Tempest* and felt that he needed to highlight his devotion by re-enacting the Hiram Abiff murder. Maybe this modern Ripper knows that the first one was an actor and is making this connection only to seem more authentic. If either is the case, though, how could we possibly know? To my knowledge, the only Ripper suspects that dabbled in acting were Walter Sickert and J.K. Stephens. There may have been others who acted; I really don't know if any other Ripper suspect was an actor. It's never been important. In addition, any connection to the Globe would be irrelevant. The original Globe had long burned down by 1888."

"What was that article that Peter had us read? The one about the religious guy?" Charlie asked.

"The article talked about Francis Thompson, a devoted Roman Catholic, and it talked about the significance of the days on which the original murders took place."

"Would that be important?" Andrews piped in.

"Only if the person we were dealing with was an extremely religious person. Not just pious either, but religious to the point where his faith was intertwined with his feelings towards the Brotherhood. If he felt the re-enactments had religious significance, and was offended that such a non-religious, maybe even counter-religious play dealing with science and the occult was a tribute to the Brotherhood, he would then be offended by the connections I made. However, that still wouldn't be enough to make him want to emulate Jack the Ripper. Unless... Maybe if he knew about the religious significance of the dates on which the prostitutes were killed, then the Ripper murders could be seen as retribution. It's an interesting possibility."

"Wait a moment," Edward said. "What document are you talking about?"

"It was from the Archive room."

"You were in the Archive room?" The Brotherhood's Grandmaster was fuming.

"Is that really important at the moment, sir?" Andrews said.

"Yes, it is important. It is important because it is a violation of the sanctity of our organization!"

"I don't give a damn at the moment. I think we finally have a motive, and if you don't want to lose more actors, I suggest you keep quiet!" Andrews roared.

"You're both yelling again," Charlie pointed out.

"I'M NOT YELLING!" shouted Edward. He took a breath and in a forced calm voice, he stammered, "You have violated our space. You accuse a Brother of committing these heinous crimes, and you expect me to remain calm?"

"Sir, if you don't mind, I do want to point out that no one is accusing the Brotherhood of supporting this," Arden tried to calm him down.

"I do mind, Ms. James. Do you have any idea what you are saying?"

"Yes, sir, I do. Just as in the first Ripper murders, I believe the Brotherhood actually stands against these killings. This is a simple case of one person misunderstanding various aspects of it and deciding to take matters into his own hands."

"And HOW can we find these things out with YOU telling us not to look at EVIDENCE!" Andrews yelled.

"And just what am I supposed to do?" came Edward's retort. "Sit back and wait for you to invade my Lodge yet again? Let you take sacred symbols and use them to publicly expose—"

"No, sir," Arden interrupted angrily. Her voice forced both men to stop their arguments and listen. "I don't intend to publicly expose anything. I respect your Brotherhood, and I would not do or say anything that could damage it. I believe in what you stand for. I respect the freedoms you offer, and the assistance you give to one another."

"If that is the case," came Edward's terse reply, "how can you stand here and accuse a Brother of these murders?"

"Because a Brother is responsible for these murders. Not the Brotherhood, but a Brother. Possibly two Brothers, but in any case, not the Brotherhood."

Edward faded back into a nearby chair. He had run out of energy. He had spent the last twenty-four hours trying to save his organization as well as his production. He had not allowed himself to mourn with his actors or for his niece and had run out of energy. There was nothing left to say.

"If you please, sir," Arden leaned in closely and spoke into his ear. "We do have one thing that we are going to try; something that would catch whoever is doing this."

"And that is?" Edward asked quietly.

"What are you telling him?" demanded Andrews.

"Andrews, you will just have to trust me on this one. There is something which I think that Edward here needs to be aware of. It is something that I do not feel comfortable announcing in a theatre packed with people." Arden looked Andrews square in the face.

Andrews looked around. "They are all police officers. There is no audience here. Dammit, girl, whatever you have to say, you will say to both of us."

"Very well, but you will have to come with Charlie and me."

"Agreed," Andrews said.

With that, Arden and Charlie led Andrews, Edward, and two other officers out of the Globe towards the London Bridge tube stop. As they walked, Charlie leaned in and whispered to Arden, "Are you sure you know what you're doing?"

"No, but someone had to do something, and we certainly weren't getting anything done standing around yelling at each other. I think this has to be the best way."

He nodded. "Well, I have faith in you. Just don't leave me alone with those two. I think they might kill each other, and anyone who gets in between them."

Arden looked at the faces of the two men who were stomping along behind her.

"You got that right. I don't think either of us should be around when the gloves come back out."

## Chapter 43

**"That's a valiant flea that dares eat his breakfast on the lip of a lion." - *Henry V***

Peter had not gone to the Globe with everyone else. He deduced that Alec's attack fell short of the mark and that Alec would be in trouble for not having killed him. Someone knew that Peter was not a member of the Brotherhood and wanted to make sure he was out of the picture. However, they had picked the wrong guy. They knew that Peter would show up at the next crime scene, so by making sure the 'next crime scene' was not what should have been next, they could commit both murders and re-enact the full activities of the Elizabeth Stride case. The downfall had been Alec's ineptitude. Peter could see the fear in Alec's eyes as he swung the knife. It was a clumsy swing, the object missing its target by too far a distance for such a close encounter. Alec had missed. Peter had gotten away, and now the architect of this mess would know that the police were hunting for Alec.

The most important thing was making sure that Arden was safe. She had sworn not to leave Charlie's side. Peter tried to ignore the twinge of jealousy that thought caused. She's better off, he said to himself. Charlie's a good guy. He'll take care of her; not that she needs taking care of.

"She was just an assignment. She still is, and I'll be damned if anything 'appens to her," he grumbled as he raced down the twisted streets.

Peter just hoped that Billingsworth had upheld his end of the deal. They could not take the jar out of the archive room, but they had come up with a solution. When

Billingsworth had first come up with the idea, Peter thought it would involve DNA samples or something. However, that would take too long, as Arden pointed out, and might only provide them with the identities of the women who had lost the organs. They already knew that part. This was much better. It did go against the Code, as Billingsworth had put it, but not as much as if they had removed something from the room. That was not allowed. Period.

Peter remembered Arden's look of surprise when he removed the pin from her jacket; the surprise of it still being there rather than the recall of a gift. It had a Masonic symbol on it and had been a present when they were dating. He had pinned it on her coat and she left it there. He was sure that she had no idea the pin contained an audio/video device. This, of course, was because she was under surveillance, and Peter needed to keep track of her. Admittedly, the audio part had been more handy, but there were moments when he had turned on his little video screen. He smiled to himself when he thought of all the things he had seen through that camera.

Nevertheless, when Billingsworth suggested planting a camera of sorts on the original Ripper jar, Peter's mind started swelling. The pin would go unnoticed. It had the right symbol, and he placed it in such a way that any activity, such as removing the other jar in order to place new objects inside of it, would be visible. Then he contacted Andrews and told him to turn on the police feed for the camera. Andrews did not know what he was looking at (other than Peter's waving and smiling face). In fact, when the group left the room, total darkness filled the camera screen. It was not until a hooded figure with a torch entered the archive room that the lens of the tiny camera came back to life.

No one noticed it. Mostly because no one had been paying attention. Peter had been using it, to be sure, but the camera at headquarters had been out of use since Arden was ruled out as a suspect. Even the recent events had not prompted anyone other than Peter to remember the pin. As he had only been using the audio feed, his video receiver was safe in his house. It would be better to take a look at any images it recorded today in Scotland Yard anyway while he was there.

Peter entered police headquarters and headed towards the surveillance room.

"Hey, mate," he said to Tom, the guard on duty.

"Peter, lad. Fancy seeing you round these parts. Thought you'd given up on the little lady."

"I have, Tom. Been usin' the camera fur somthink else."

"Got a new lead, have you now?"

"It's a bit like that."

"Well, then, what can I do for you?"

"Thought I'd take a look at number 26. It's the same ol' camera, but I set it up new today, yeah?"

"Ah, yeah. Been wondering about that one. Is that the one with the head?"

"The what?" Peter felt a chill go up his spine.

"The head. In the dark room. Could barely see it myself. Had to look pretty close." He went over to one of the screens and fiddled with buttons until the image appeared. Sure enough, it was the archive room. The camera was staring at a large jar. A candle was placed next to it on a table. It was the archive room, and sure enough, Peter could just make out the silhouette of a head placed neatly in the jar.

"Bollocks!" Peter cursed.

Then he picked up the phone. First, he called Andrews but got no answer. He didn't bother leaving a message. After thinking for a moment, he picked up the phone again and called Billingsworth.

## Chapter 44

**"Many Strokes, though with a little axe, hew down and fell the hardest-timber'd oak."**

***- Henry VI Part III***

Arden and Charlie led the party into the underground station and instructed Edward to ensure they were all dropped off at the secret tube stop. He had not been happy about this, but at least they did not need to violate any more of the space than was absolutely necessary. The driver's carriage was not built for so many extra passengers; so needless to say, it was not a comfortable journey.

"Everyone in?" Charlie asked jokingly. "I'm sure we can fit a few more and some pets if anyone has any. Arden? Any dogs, cats, goldfish maybe? What do you think? A camel?"

"Yes, a whole farm's worth, just left them at home. Sorry. I'll remember next time we plan on squeezing into a five-foot by two-foot space."

"I'm glad someone's finding humor in this situation," snapped Andrews. "Stop hitting me, you bastard!"

"Then get out of my way!" Edward yelled. "Anyway, lay off him. The boy's just trying to lighten the mood. I for one would like to be distracted enough to forget that I am smashed into a four-foot space in an underground hole."

"Did someone just defend me?" whispered Charlie.

"Don't get too excited; you never know how long it will last," came Arden's reply.

Andrews had been set off again. “It’s always about you, isn’t it? You quite obviously have no idea how serious this is.”

“On the contrary, I am more than well aware of all the ramifications of both this little journey, and more importantly, what will happen if we do not successfully find what we are looking for.”

“This carriage is far too small for you to be screaming, you—”

“Here’s our stop,” Charlie quickly and thankfully pointed out as the carriage came to a halt.

The group tumbled out of the train and onto the makeshift platform. Edward took a flashlight out of a cabinet near the door.

“I didn’t notice that before,” Charlie said.

“You shouldn’t have been here at all before. I should hope there are many things other than a flashlight that you did not notice.”

“See,” whispered Arden, “I told you it wouldn’t last.”

Charlie snickered.

“I’m glad someone’s finding this amusing,” grumbled Andrews again.

“Would you lot just shut it? Follow me.”

Edward led the way to the archive room. However, when they got close to the door, they noticed a light coming from inside.

“Shhh,” Edward cautioned.

They crept towards the archive door. Edward shifted so that he was holding his flashlight, ready to strike whoever came out. He threw open the door.

"Billingsworth, Peter! What the devil is going on here?"

The two people were sitting at the table. Silence filled the room.

"Well?" inquired Edward tersely. "Out with it. Why may I ask are you here?"

They looked at the new visitors. Billingsworth spoke first.

"It seems we have a bit of a problem."

"Oh, good. I was worried that we were having a dinner party," Edward said sarcastically.

Billingsworth moved a black cloth that had been covering a large object. Lifting it, he revealed the jar it had covered, which stood in the middle of the table. In the jar was most definitely a human head.

"It's Alec," Peter said.

The others crowded around and, sure enough, Alec's head had been cut off at the neck and placed in the jar.

As the group stared at this gruesome discovery, Peter spoke.

"I went back to look at the tape, yeah? And the camera was lookin' at this lovely sight."

"There was a camera?" Edward asked.

"We put it here last night," Arden explained.

"What camera?"

"I had given this lovely lady a charm with an A/V device back when we thought she might've been involved in somethink. It'd been off for ages, but when we were in here and found the jar with the new Ripper parts, we thought'd be a good idea to keep the camera here and see who has been doin' this."

"Did you watch the rest of the tape?" Andrews asked.

"Yessir, Gov. Got it right here on me DVD. No sound though. Seems we 'ad some problems wiv the feed."

Peter took out a laptop from his bag and hit play. A hooded figure holding a candle flashed to life on the screen. He sat at one end of the table. Peter fast-forwarded.

"He sat there fur a bit till someone came."

Peter stopped fast-forwarding when Alec entered the room. Without sound, all they could tell was that the figure stood up and walked to Alec, placing his hand on Alec's shoulder. The figure took out a knife and plunged it into Alec. Alec fell to the floor, mouthing something. Once he was dead, the figure stood back and stared at his handiwork. He turned towards the camera and moved as if he was going to pick up the jar next to it. However, the eager hand felt around the shelf space next to the jar as if it was looking for something. After a moment, he stopped when he saw his intended target. The hand reached to the camera, lifting it from its hiding place. The screen went dark.

Peter hit fast forward. The clock on the screen fast-forwarded ten minutes, then fifteen, then twenty.

Finally, the image returned and revealed the new jar with the head in it, sitting square on the table. A candle was placed next to it, and the scene that Peter had first seen on the monitor in the surveillance room became clear.

The film stopped.

Silence filled the room. After a few minutes, Charlie asked the looming question, "Where's the rest of him?"

"I wondered the same thing, I had a look around, and it's not here, that's for sure," Peter said.

"Edward, I do not want to cause you problems, but this room is now a murder scene," Andrews said gently.

"Of course you want to cause problems, but if it makes any difference, I am well aware of that little fact. Scotland Yard will have my full co-operation, I assure you." Edward looked at Arden and Charlie. "Why did you want me to come here?"

"For the same reason we set up the camera. To show you this other jar."

"It is new; I was in here myself the other day, and nothing was different. Then today, this appears," Billingsworth echoed in agreement.

"The killer has been placing parts of these new victims in a jar next to the old ones," Arden explained. "That's why we set up the camera. Billingsworth wouldn't let us take anything out, so we figured this way we could have a look in."

"The tape is so very dark. If only we had a good shot of the bastard's face," Andrews sighed.

"Maybe we do," Arden said hopefully. "Rewind that tape."

"Your wish is me command," Peter said.

When they got to the part when Alec was stabbed, Arden told him to let it play. She watched, rewound, and watched again. Then she let it play as the figure came over to the camera. The hood hung deeply over his face. A chin with traces of a beard was visible.

"Damn. It's no good. He seems to know where the camera is and makes sure that we can't see his face."

As the others moved away, Charlie got in closer to the tape. There was something...

"Wait a second," Charlie murmured. He played the same scene over again. He watched the man's chin and his hand. Then he rewound back and watched something else. He paused the tape and thought for a moment. His mind thought back on all he had seen. Then he remembered the *Tempest* poster in the office. Andrews had said there were no *Tempest* posters anywhere. But there had been one. Had he checked the office? Was that the one that had been in the Alley? And why had there been no camera in here before? Who knew they had put one in? He played Alec's death scene back one more time. There it is! His eyes grew large as the realization materialized in his mind. It's there... and that man, he is moving so... Suddenly it all made sense. But what could he say? In an instant, he had a plan. Charlie turned, eyes wide, and stared at the group.

"We have to act fast."

## Chapter 45

**"Not that I lov'd Caesar less, but that I lov'd Rome more." - *Julius Caesar***

The Benefactor knelt at the altar of the Lodge. This was a holy place where he could ask forgiveness and be granted salvation. Soon, it would become clear to everyone else. As he prayed, a loud creak echoed from the secret door. He looked over, startled, and acknowledged the Man who walked in through the side door.

"Good work, my Brother," came the Man's voice.

The Benefactor nodded and stood up. "How much time do we have?"

"It will be soon."

"Do they know?" asked the Benefactor.

"No. Stupid Americans."

The Man knelt down next to the Benefactor and prayed. The two had met nearly six years before, at the initiation ceremony. It was a great honor to be allowed into the unique circle that made up the Grand Lodge. In addition, both men were devout in their beliefs. Such piety had become too rare. They would go to the meetings together after church. Soon, they were going out together to the pub after the meetings. They would talk for hours about the Lodge, and about those people who didn't understand and who couldn't embrace the true faith. The Benefactor had come across the books first, but they had angered both of them. The two men spoke endlessly about finding a way to stop the heretics from publishing such nonsense. They even sent anonymous letters using various famous quotes, threatening to do something about it. They always remembered to include the Brotherhood, as it was sacred to them.

The Man had begun to research Jack the Ripper on a whim. He realized that the dates of the murders, and the symbols of which Stephen Knight wrote, proved that the Brotherhood was really trying to dispel the garbage lining the streets of London. The garbage that tried to threaten them. Fancy that. The Benefactor suggested using some of the research in the letters. They hoped that by writing, the press might get wind of the truth and do away with the heretics. When nothing happened, their frustration only grew.

Then the Benefactor read Arden's book. Here was the ultimate insult. All the research and years of frustration boiled over, and their plan was set into motion.

The Man rose from the floor. "I've enjoyed watching them. I must say, it's been frightfully entertaining seeing them struggle."

"Yes, but we cannot forget what we want. Always keep your focus, my Brother."

"Ah, yes. I have written the Times. Once she is dead, the papers will descend upon us. We can finally regain our rightful power and make it clear that no one should ever dare presume to trifle with the Order."

The Benefactor smiled and nodded. He held out his hand to the Man. Once the sign was complete, they left the safety of the Lodge to complete their task.

## Chapter 46

## "More Matter with Less Art." - *Hamlet*

At Bankside, the students were finishing breakfast and getting ready to meet their professors. Charlie and Arden showed up just in time to see Hendry alert the group that they should get to work. Charlie inhaled the familiar fragrance of bacon and took a minute to think longingly about food.

"Mmm, breakfast," he murmured.

"You can grab something if you are hungry," Arden whispered. "It's still there. Better hurry, though; they're clearing it away. Besides, it'd be a great way of giving him the bait. He's bound to come up to you."

"But if I go in there... Mary Jo might be there."

Arden thought about this for a minute. "I guess we'll have to take that chance."

They went into the cafeteria and Charlie rushed over to the table and grabbed a banana and a box of cereal. As he did, Mary Jo and Hendry both came up to him. Mary Jo got there first.

"Now, Charlie. That was not very nice of you, lying to me like that."

"Huh?"

"The Queen never did come to that crime scene. I waited the whole time. That nice deputy told me I didn't have to. He even offered to take me in to get me off the streets. Wasn't that nice?"

"Take you in? Like put you in jail?" Charlie cringed.

"Jail? No silly. He said that Americans like me shouldn't be let loose around London, and that if I knew what was good for me, I'd go back... oh what did he say... something about going back to America and staying there forever. There was a murder and all. And it was so cold! In June! Imagine that. Him trying to protect me. These guys are just as sweet as pudding!"

"What did you say to him?"

"Well, I told that detective that I just couldn't thank him enough and that I'd be just fine waiting for the Queen all by my lonesome. Then Mr. H here came over and brought me all the way back here to Bankside. He also said he didn't want me to get hurt."

Hendry raised an eyebrow as he replied, "I believe my exact words, Ms. White, were that although I would love for you to find the killer and let him have his way with you, or for the Queen to throw you into the deepest pit in the British Empire, I do not have a good enough lawyer to justify misplacing one of my students. Not even one as American as yourself."

"Oh, you are too cute!" Mary Jo giggled.

"Yes, well, why don't you go off and look for Princess Diana. I'm sure your professor wouldn't mind. You can come back once you've gotten her autograph," Hendry muttered.

"Really?" Mary Jo squealed. Then she turned to a group of students sitting at a nearby table and yelled, "Come on y'all! We're looking for royalty!"

She ran over and forced the group to get up and walk with her out of the cafeteria.

"Does she know that Princess Diana is deceased?" Charlie volunteered.

"Really now, that is not the sort of thing one tells such a girl. It will just make her search a tad longer. I'm sure her instructor will not mind a brief spell of peace and quiet," Hendry replied.

Charlie snickered. Hendry did have a sense of humor.

At that Hendry turned his attention back to Charlie. "Did you oversleep? Must have had a busy night."

"It was pretty busy, thank you. Busy, but interesting," Charlie replied with a mouth full of food.

"You think lounging around at crime scenes is good fun, boy?"

"Who said I was lounging around?" he retorted with a mouth full of banana. "All in a night's work. Got to write a play, you know."

Arden came over to the buffet table. "Charlie, there you are. We better get going. Lots to do. Good morning, Richard."

"Ms. James. How are you enjoying your amateur detective work?"

"It keeps me busy. Come on, Charlie, we'd better go. Has anyone ever told you to chew?"

"Mmmhmm," came the response.

"And just where are you going, my dear?"

"Well, Andrews has a lead on last night's case. It seems the murderer was sloppy and left something that identified him at the crime scene. I'd say this whole thing will be wrapped up in no time."

"Identified him? And what was that, may I ask?"

"I don't know; Andrews didn't tell me. But we have to go meet him now, and he's sure to have the whole thing done and the guy caught by lunch time."

"Yes, all right then. Where are you going?"

"To where Mary Kelly was killed."

Arden and Charlie left and headed over towards Whitechapel.

"Do you think he's following us?" Arden whispered after a while.

"I know he's following us. He is lucky he never chose a career as a spy. He's not very good at sneaking around."

"We need to slow down; we're walking way too fast."

"I don't know about you, but I am slightly nervous, and I always walk fast when I'm nervous."

"What have you got to be nervous about? Everything is rosy. Decapitated heads in jars, dead women lying on the streets, body parts stored for posterity. I'd say you have absolutely no reason in the world to be nervous."

Now it was Charlie's turn to laugh. "Has anyone ever told you that you have a great sense of humor?"

"I don't know, there was this one guy, but he put a camera in a piece of jewelry he gave to me so I'm not sure how much I believe him," Arden said sarcastically.

"You know what I think?"

"What do you think?"

"I think you need to date someone who is not British."

"I thought I was."

"Yes, I believe you are. Someone younger, slightly immature, but incredibly brave, intelligent, and devastatingly handsome." Charlie stood up straight.

"And modest, right?"

"Absolutely."

Arden felt sure Charlie could hear how loud her heart was pounding. Her head began swirling as if it was trying to keep up with the heartbeats.

"I hate to put a damper on this conversation, which I am really enjoying, by the way, but we are almost there. What do we do ow?" Arden asked.

"Let's hope that your ex is where he's supposed to be. Everything else is in place."

"I sure hope you're right about this," she said.

"That makes two of us."

"How reassuring." Arden raised an eyebrow.

"Relax. I promise, whatever happens, I won't let anyone hurt you." He stopped for a moment and took her hand. Looking directly into her eyes he spoke again. "I promise."

"I believe you," Arden nodded.

Charlie kissed her gently.

"And you know," Arden said, "I won't let anyone hurt you either."

Charlie laughed and pulled her into an embrace. "Good. I was worried about that."

After a moment, he continued, "Come on. We have to go. Give me your phone; I'll call Andrews."

## Chapter 47

**"Hold up, you sluts, your aprons mountant." - *Timon of Athens***

Peter stood alone in the alley called "White's Row." It was directly across from an oversized industrial-looking parking garage. Where Mary Kelly was killed. Arden was right. It would be very hard to replicate a killing that took place in a room that wasn't there anymore. Somehow, death in a parking garage just wouldn't be the same. Especially one that was filled with cars. How many people use this lot? Okay, focus, he said to himself. He thought back to what Arden told them while they were in the archive room staring at Alec's head.

"Mary Kelly's was the most gruesome killing. She was in pieces. They cut out her heart and her entire abdominal area. Pieces of her lay strewn around the bed. Her breasts were severed and placed beside her body. Her face was cut to pieces as well. She was only recognizable by her eyes and her clothes. This helped foster a theory that she was not the one who was killed."

"What do you mean, she wasn't killed? You just said she was in pieces," Peter had asked.

"I said the body was in pieces. Here are the facts: she was killed on November seventh. At about three or four in the morning, people who lived above her heard a cry of 'murder.' However, two witnesses who knew her both swore they saw her that morning between 8:30 and 9:30. Her body wasn't found until later in the day. When it was found, her door was locked. In addition, the kettle over her fireplace had melted, indicating a huge fire, strong enough to melt the iron kettle. Yet, no one allegedly saw light streaming from her room."

"Her door was locked? How did—"

"Her window was broken. It had been for some time and it was right next to the door. There was enough space for someone to stick his hand through the hole in the window and grab the handle of the door. It was odd that after cutting up a person, there was no record of blood being on the handle, and you would think that whoever it was, if he didn't have a key, would have had to stick his hand back through the window to lock it from the inside. This is one of the things that prompts the theory that her lover committed the murder, but it also encourages the theory that she was not the one in her room that night—that she had let a friend stay in her room, and it was her friend who was actually killed. Mary Kelly returned early in the morning to find the horrible scene. She changed out of her clothes and put on the clothes her friend had taken off before going to sleep that night. After locking the door and heading out, she was recognized by the two witnesses. Once news got around that she was dead, the real Mary Kelly left town. There is no proof for any of this, but it is a viable theory."

"There's no proof to anythink, but that's not really important, now, is it?" Peter replied.

Peter's worst fears centered around the substitution for the Mary Kelly victim. He tried not to think about it, but now the truth seemed unavoidable. The next murder victim did not have to be a witch from Macbeth. It would go along with the theory that the real Mary Kelly had not died. Arden pointed out that anyone could die if the present murderer supported this theory. The pattern was broken. They all knew that Arden was the object of interest. She had been the one whose thoughts on symbols and Shakespeare was the catalyst for these copycat killings. Planting her book at the crime scenes ensured her involvement, and while the focus was on the Globe and the actresses there, the killer would be following Arden's movements. To finally get to the bottom of this, she would have to be at the next murder scene before the next murder took place. She would need to use herself as bait. Otherwise, the trail would literally disappear.

The strange part had been Andrews. He had given Peter strict orders to go to the Globe in case any more problems came up there. It was only when Charlie had pulled Peter aside that the order made sense. Peter knew Charlie was right. It was Arden from the beginning. Disregarding Andrews' orders, Peter raced to White's Row. That's where he needed to be. There was no way he'd mess this up. He would be there first. He would save her.

This alley had an assortment of crevices, all of which were well hidden. They were all somehow familiar, as if Peter had been here in his dreams. He knew this alley. His family had moved out to the country after his mother had been killed. He shut out that part of his life, except for the dreams, but now... He looked around. It was a coincidence, he knew, but he had been here before. He came here every night when he closed his eyes and chased them down the street, clinging onto his brother's hand. He picked an alcove where he had a clear view of the street, but he knew that no one could possibly see him until they were already too close. This was where they hid, and now, this was where he would strike back.

The Benefactor walked towards the parking garage. Such a pity that such an ugly building had replaced such an important landmark. Nevertheless, it would have to do. He had been waiting for this. Soon enough they would be there, and everyone would finally know the truth. Retribution would be his. They would regret the blasphemous sins committed against the Brotherhood. A few feet from White's Row, he knelt down and prayed. This was a holy site, after all. He mustn't forget the significance of this moment or those who perished in the name of the Order. He found a nearby doorway and stood waiting. It would not be long now.

## Chapter 48

**"Truth makes all things plain." – *A Midsummer Night's Dream***

Charlie and Arden walked down the street towards the site. "Are you sure we know what we are doing?" Arden asked.

"I hope so. Either that or my mother made me watch too many episodes of *Murder She Wrote."*

"I loved that show!"

"Of course you did," Charlie snickered. "So did I, actually. Don't tell anyone. Guilty pleasure."

They were about 15 feet from White's Row when Arden stopped walking.

"Charlie," Arden said, "I want to thank you again. Really. I know I sound like a broken record, but you didn't have to be here or get involved in any of this. But you did, and I don't know what I'd have done without you."

Charlie stared at Arden. He felt a need to protect her. He knew that somehow all this had happened for a reason. All of a sudden, he became conscious of the world around him. What should he do now? After all this is over, would he have to go back?

"Look, I'm not very good at this part, but do you... I mean, after we, ya know, save the world or whatever... do you want to go out sometime? With me?"

Charlie felt embarrassed hearing the words come out of his mouth. However, all Arden had to do was smile, and he knew it would all be all right.

"Are you asking me out? Like on a date?"

"Yes, exactly like a date—a real one with no possibility of sudden death."

Arden laughed. "Whatever would we do?"

"I don't know, but I'm sure we could figure something out."

Arden nodded. "I'm sure we can find something entertaining. Normal, not life-threatening. Yes, Charlie. I'd like that. I'd like that very much."

It started to rain as he leaned over and kissed her gently. Arden felt her whole body melt into his arms, and for a moment, everything else vanished.

A strangely familiar voice broke through the moment. "Well, isn't that lovely."

"Winston!" Arden said, taking out her umbrella.

"Waiting for you. You are right on time. Good job; you always were punctual."

"What do you want, Winston?"

"What do I want? I want so many things. Peace, love, but most of all, I would like retribution for the violations you have inflicted upon my Brotherhood."

Arden suddenly realized that Winston was holding a long knife, so sharp that it seemed to cut through the raindrops.

"It's you, isn't it?" she said. "You're the one who's been committing all these murders. You lied about my dissertation being stolen, and then made it look like Alec was the one behind it all."

"And when he didn't kill Peter, you killed him," Charlie accused.

"My children, it is such a pity that you would not take the good advice given to you and stayed out of this. You had such a bright future, and from the looks of it, quite a good night planned. It pains me to have to do this, but ashes to ashes."

He started to walk towards them.

"You think we are just going to stand here while you try to kill us?"

"Yes, I do." The voice came from behind them. It was Andrews. He stood still except for the pistol that he pulled from his jacket.

"I wouldn't do that if I were you." Peter popped out of his corner. He had been surprised enough to see the hooded figure step out of a doorway, but Andrews? The kid had been right.

"Peter, what the devil are you doing here? I gave you strict orders..."

"Which I chose t'ignore, Gov. Me humblest apologies, but it seems I'm better use over 'ere just at present."

He pulled the safety off his gun, which was pointed straight at Andrews' head.

Winston, meanwhile, was standing now with his knife out, ready to slice at anyone who came near him. Andrews' gun had been wavering between Arden and Charlie, but now stayed focused on Arden.

"Peter, I'm sure you understand that no matter what you do, I must kill your former girlfriend. In fact, Winston must do it. The cycle has to be finished, and we unfortunately need a Mary Jane Kelly. The rest of you are incidental, but if you died in the line of duty, no one would think the slightest on it."

"Yessir, and if you died in the line of duty, no one'd be bothered. And if you so much as touch a hair on either of these twos' heads, that'd be exactly what would happen. Sir."

Peter spat at Andrews as he said the word 'sir.'

"That, my boy, was highly uncalled for. But as it is, it seems as though we have come to a stalemate."

"Not exactly," came the response, this time from a new voice directly behind Andrews. Hendry had arrived.

"Richard!" Arden didn't know what to do. One gun on her, two guns on Andrews. Something had to happen. She looked at Charlie, who was also assessing the situation. Their eyes met for a moment, and then the madness started. Arden stepped as hard as she could on Andrews' foot, smacking him on the head with her umbrella at the same time. The jolt forced him to drop his arm and bend down in pain. Charlie promptly punched him as hard as he could. From behind, Hendry ran over and tried to grab Andrews' gun. The ground was too slippery, forcing the men to fall on top of each other as they struggled to grab a hold of it. Charlie and Arden ran towards Peter who had, in the confusion, managed to attack Winston, forcing him to drop his knife. A gunshot went off, and Arden saw Hendry's body lurch backwards. Then immediately, as though on cue, a chorus of sirens closed in on them. Peter was caught off guard by the noise, which allowed Winston to free himself and lunge for his knife. He swung frantically, slicing Peter in the gut, and began to run, but his legs were too lame, and the ground too slick. In an instant,

Winston found himself cornered by the mass of police cars that had blocked off the street. A second shot rang out, whizzing by Charlie's ear. Charlie turned to see Andrews racing towards him. At once, the heavens seemed to open, and what had been a light rain became a downpour.

"Over here, you bloody wanker!" screamed Peter through the din of the rain on the cobblestones.

Andrews turned just in time to see a now blood-soaked and waterlogged Peter fire right at him. Andrews' body lunged backwards, dropping his gun in the process. Charlie skidded over and grabbed it. Andrews fell to the ground. Charlie found his balance and tried to steady his arm, which was nervously waving Andrews' gun around. The sirens and the storm overtook all of his senses.

The police moved on the scene quickly, and from nowhere, a calm voice told Charlie to give him the gun. Charlie swung around, clutching the pistol. Billingsworth had his hand out, and gently took it from Charlie's grasp.

"It's over now. Don't worry, son. It's over."

**Chapter 49**

**"Haste still pays haste, and leisure answers leisure, Like doth quit like, and measure still for measure." - *Measure for Measure***

Charlie and Arden sat silently, wrapped in towels, in the all-too-familiar Scotland Yard office. Pacing around the room was a thoroughly confused Edward Filbin.

Billingsworth was still surrounded by a number of officers who were all busily jotting down their orders. When they had gone, he settled into the desk chair and stared at his visitors.

"I want to thank you, my boy. I had a feeling there was someone from the inside calling the shots, but I had not realized that it was Andrews. How did you figure it out?"

"Yes and, while you're at it, do you mind telling me what the hell's going on?" Edward piped in.

Charlie took a deep breath. It was his turn to answer questions.

"I didn't realize it until Alec's head was in that jar. The pin with the camera was really not noticeable. There were tons of things with that symbol on it all over that bookcase. In the video, the man with the hood looked directly at it. It was as though he knew what he was looking at. He seemed to know the pin had a camera in it. How would he know that unless someone told him? I thought about it and realized that the only people who knew about the camera were those of us in the room when we put it there and Andrews."

"What about Winston? How did you know it was him?"

"Two things. The man in the video was moving in a really strange way. There was one person who moved that slowly. Winston had a distinctive limp. Not only that, but the whole bit with the *Tempest* poster. When we got to the Globe, Andrews was upset because he couldn't find any *Tempest* posters around. How strange is that? I mean, they put on that show recently, and posters from every season were scattered all over that building. He even described the poster that we had seen at the crime scene. It reminded me that it was like the one I had seen somewhere before. That's when I remembered that there had been one of those posters in Winston's office. Also, the specific poster I had seen earlier in the office was exactly the same one that had the writing on it. It was numbered as though it was a special edition. I remembered looking at it the day before and wondering how strange it was to make a publicity poster limited edition."

"You really did watch too much *Murder She Wrote,*" joked Arden.

Charlie smiled. "I didn't put it together until we saw the video of Alec dying. He was mouthing something when he was falling. He was mouthing a name. I watched it a few times and realized that he was mouthing 'Winston.' Another thing was the guy never took off his hood. He knew where to look for the camera without taking off the huge hood, and he knew somehow which angles he could turn without letting the camera get a good look at his face. The only thing that was visible was his chin.

"After that it was easy to put together that it was Winston who had killed Alec. However, it must not have been Winston who committed the Elizabeth Stride copycat killing because Alec was obviously surprised at the face under the hood. Alec was at that crime scene with someone else. Therefore, there must have been two people involved. That's how the double murders could happen at the same time. Winston killed Eddowes; Andrews killed Stride. I was trying to figure out who the second person was. I honestly didn't know yet. I thought it might have been you, Mr. Billingsworth, but I was also really wary of Andrews. All that stuff about not wanting surveillance in the archives room? It seemed too strange. There were so many things that made him a bit too shady. He had all those files in his office, yet he kept asking Arden all those questions. And then, I remembered again that there were only a few people who knew about the camera."

"Again, us, and Andrews..."

"Yep. When we were all in that room it started to come together. I came up with the plan, knowing that if Andrews was involved, he would do something to stop us. Then Andrews told Peter to go to the Globe and see if anything new was going on there. That made no sense. We were all headed over to the Mary Kelly location. Why would he want Peter to go someplace else? I stopped Peter before he left and told him to ignore the order and hide at the Kelly scene. Peter had found the order strange, as well, and agreed to find a place he could hide that would be out of the way so that even whoever met us there wouldn't see him."

"I told him about White's Row. It's a creepy alley right across from the parking lot. I guess he found it okay because he went on ahead and got into place," Arden agreed.

"Peter knew the alley well," Billingsworth interrupted.

"What do you mean?" asked Arden.

"When Peter was five, his family—mother, father, and little brother—were living in Whitechapel, not far from Spitalfields Market. One day, when his father was out, some men showed up. Two of them dragged his mother from their flat, leaving their colleagues to watch the boys. Peter was a feisty lad even as a boy. He somehow managed to escape with his brother. They ran after the men who had taken his mother. When they found her, in White's Row, she was dying. They called for help, but they were too late. She was dead by the time the police came. His father had owed money to the men, and they were taking their revenge. When the father heard about what happened, he ran off in disgrace, leaving the boys to their grandparents.

"I... I didn't know," Arden whispered.

"No one did. At the time, of course, it was in all the papers, but the boys' names were kept private for their own protection."

"I feel awful. I wish I had known. I could have helped." Arden shook her head.

Billingsworth smiled. "You have. More than you know. I'm sure you'll find that Peter is just fine. Now, my boy," he said turning back to Charlie. "I want to know what happened after you talked to Peter."

"Well, then we went along with the plan I had talked about with Andrews," Charlie continued slowly. "I figured Hendry was somehow involved. He was showing up at all these murder scenes without explanation. It was easy to convince Andrews that I thought it was him. I told Andrews that Arden and I would lure Hendry to the Kelly scene, and then he could wait for us to capture him before he tried to kill Arden. Andrews must have thought that Hendry wouldn't go along with it. He knew who was responsible, and it wasn't Hendry.

"Hendry, however, did fall for it, and followed us to the scene. He wasn't involved in the killings, but he was more than interested in knowing who was. We didn't know if he would help us or hurt us, but we did know that Andrews would surely tell Winston to be there waiting."

"How did you know that there would be backup officers?" Edward asked. "If you knew that Andrews was involved, then you could hardly have told Peter to radio for backup."

"That was the hard part. We figured that Andrews wouldn't expect Peter to be there, since Peter usually followed orders, so Andrews would just expect him to go where he was told. Peter used a pay phone to call headquarters. He told them to keep it quiet and not use any signal that Andrews might have heard. I don't know what else he told them, but since they showed up, I'm assuming they just believed him. What I don't know, Mr. B., is how you are involved in all this." Charlie stopped talking and stared intently at Billingsworth.

Billingsworth smiled. "Ah, so it's my turn. Well, I suppose you deserve the whole story. I've been involved from the start. As I told you, about five years ago, I got wind that there was new activity with regards to the Ripper files. I'm the archivist. I know everything. I kept my eyes open, and soon realized that Winston, who is an upper-echelon

Mason, and extremely religious, was collecting new information on the Ripper murders and storing it in the archive room.

"Winston had been in trouble with the Brotherhood in the past. He had, at one time, been a highly revered Mason. However, upon his initiation as Master Mason, his personality started to change. He became even more fervently religious and seemed to include the Brotherhood in his piety. I had been watching him for some time before this trouble started. You see, one must not confuse Brotherhood with divinity. We work together for each other, and for the good of the Lodge. We do not discuss God. Each of us stands firm within our own beliefs, but those beliefs are rarely the same. There have been times in the past when Brothers have looked to the Masters for salvation. It simply doesn't work that way. We do not offer anything beyond the safe reaches of mankind.

"It may surprise you to know that I do not spend all my time working the archives. I have been an undercover detective for some time. Few know that fact. I have managed to keep my work... under wraps, shall we say. Most of the Brothers don't know my actual profession. Some think I am simply a man of leisure. That is true to a certain extent, but years ago I made a deal with a friend of mine and have kept my bargain ever since. Andrews would not have known because I don't work for Andrews. Or Scotland Yard. I work directly for the Home Office. I knew Andrews, but only because he also was a Mason of the same rank as Winston. Both of these ranks outweigh yourself, sir." He looked directly at Edward.

"I'm Grandmaster of the Lodge. How would I not have known them?"

"It is the nature of the organization. There are many levels which overshadow others. They are all shrouded in their own mystery, and no one from one level to another even knows of the existence of those above him. Yes, you are Grandmaster of the Lodge; of this Lodge and the Third Degree. There are levels above that. There are district levels, which outrank each other. They have separate meetings, separate oaths, and do separate work. At each level there is a master. That master is eventually initiated to the next level, which was previously unknown to him. Many have written books, but they manage only to touch on the surface. Keeping each other in the dark is vital to this organization. It is how we have survived for so many centuries. You cannot talk about what you do not know."

"And what level are you, sir?"

"That is something which you will never know. What I can tell you is what happened after I discovered Winston's curious behavior."

"Enlighten us."

"I did not know what he was up to, but I did report to my superiors that something was beginning to tick, so to speak. They alerted Andrews that mysterious activity related to the Globe Theatre needed to be investigated. Andrews was given the original Ripper files, and began investigating, so to speak. He recruited Peter, who faked membership in the Brotherhood to get more information; all of which I was secretly feeding him. He did not know me as anything but the archivist, of course, but I made sure he found things. Winston, meanwhile, knew he was being watched. He did not know by whom, so he became Alec's benefactor and used him as an unwilling pawn. Winston, in his confusion, felt that the sanctity of the Brotherhood was being violated. Alec was easy to manipulate. When Winston got wind of your research, activity began to speed up. He got together with fellow master and religious zealot Andrews. They both felt the Brotherhood was a religion and justified their actions as a campaign to restore the Knights to their proper place. They researched various past, misguided crusaders and came across Sir William Gull's part in the alleged Ripper conspiracy. They discussed using the Ripper murders as a religious statement, educating themselves only on the royal conspiracy theory and the significance of the original dates.

"Winston, as head of Globe Education, recognized the symbols you spoke of and began doing his own research. When your dissertation was published, it was as though hell itself had entered their world. He used the Globe and Shakespeare to try and issue a warning. When that didn't work, they decided that replicating the Ripper murders was the only way out. By leaving your dissertation at each scene, you would be involved, and then you were the intended last victim. It would all be a warning to anyone who dared speak against the Brotherhood."

"But I didn't speak against it. I'm all for it."

"They didn't see it that way. They saw you as the ultimate insult. It became imperative to get rid of you."

"I don't understand why they didn't just go after me, then."

"That would not have been effective. They didn't just want to kill you; they wanted to make a statement. Their objective was for all mankind to recognize the Masons as the 'true path.' By using such familiar icons as Shakespeare and the Ripper, they thought they would accomplish both religious martyrdom of sorts and domination within the Brotherhood. In addition, they would send out a warning to anyone attempting to trifle with what they saw as a holy order."

Arden thought for a moment. "So, my dissertation was at the scene of each crime because—"

"My dear," interrupted Billingsworth, "your little book was everything they were against—scholars exposing private rituals—while tying these two separate icons together. In addition, you being an American, a Ripperologist, a woman and a budding Shakespearean scholar embodying all the things they hated. In Winston's and Andrews' minds, your thesis justified their actions."

Edward shook his head. "I don't know what to say. They have put everything in jeopardy."

"Yes. But I wouldn't worry. These things have a way of working themselves out. For instance, there is no need to let the papers know of the motives. Damage control is already in motion, and there will be no repercussions for the Brotherhood. "

"Andrews is dead, but what of Winston?"

"He will go to jail. His trial may be a bit abbreviated, of course. There are some powerful Masons in the Justice Department."

"What about Peter? Will he be all right?" Arden asked.

"He'll be just fine. The cut was a surface wound. He'll be in hospital for a while, but he should make a full recovery. As far as the rest goes, I think he'll be just fine."

Arden nodded, understanding.

"Hendry isn't so lucky," Billingsworth continued. "He was a brave man."

"How was he involved?" asked Charlie.

"He was a Brother who worked closely enough with the Globe to know something was wrong. He was trying to get answers, which no one would give him. Unfortunately, he tried to take matters into his own hands. I'm sure he was just trying to protect you, but it ended up getting him killed."

Silence filled the room. Arden felt horrible for thinking Hendry was involved in the murders. He had practically saved her life, and Charlie's. She would always be grateful to him.

"Now, if you will excuse me," sighed Billingsworth, "I have a large amount of work to do. I will be contacting you to get a full statement, but I must ask that you keep this between us."

"Absolutely," Arden agreed.

"I wouldn't know how to tell anyone anything anyway," Charlie said.

Edward looked at Billingsworth. "I have a show to save somehow. Then I need a vacation."

"And the archive room?" asked Arden. "I still wonder about the real Ripper. The one from 1888. Do you think that those dates are important? What about some of the others? Stephens? Was he involved in the Royal conspiracy? Any conspiracy? Do you think Andrews and Winston... Did they find something in the archive room to make them look at the killings the way they did? Will we ever be able to test the body parts or the folders? What about Sickert? Was he involved? Did Gull have Sickert and Stephens murder the girls because of something to do with the Royals? Wait a second... Maybe that's it! The first Ripper... He wasn't a Mason, but he knew one... was a friend of one... They discovered something and used it to try and join the Brotherhood... like you said, and—"

"My dear," Billingsworth interrupted gently, "I know you are curious, but I must insist. The information we have must remain as it is. Buried. In the spirit of that, I have already ordered that room sealed. It is a tomb. In Alec's case, it is his grave. We found the rest of his body in the river. I have placed it in the archive room and have arranged for the entrance to be closed off forever. I am also arranging for a new archive room to be built in a place sacred to the Order. There are some things which must remain as they are. In time, the truth may reveal itself, but for the moment it is better to leave well enough alone."

**Chapter 50**

**"What's past is prologue" - *The Tempest***

Charlie and Arden walked in silence for what seemed like hours. They ended up in the familiar confines of The George pub. Exchanging a look, they went inside and ordered drinks. They sank into a booth, unable to speak. Arden sneezed.

Charlie finally broke the silence. "Bless you."

"Thanks," she replied.

"Careful you don't catch your death. What are you doing running around without your umbrella?"

"I seemed to have dropped it. Maybe that was after I whacked Andrews on the head."

"Excuses, excuses," snickered Charlie. "Well, we know that Peter won't be coming in here this time."

"Yes, that's true. I'm just glad that he'll be okay."

Charlie paused. "Were you scared?"

"You mean when there was a gun pointed at my head?"

"Yeah."

"Terrified. You were brave, though. I could never have grabbed that gun."

"Yeah, but you started everything, stepping on Andrews' foot. That took guts. I didn't know what to do," he said, staring into her eyes.

"Then I ran and hid."

Charlie shrugged. "Nobody's perfect."

"It's so strange; I mean, the last forty-eight hours of my life have been all about the Ripper. But not the real one. Not the one that I had set out to discover. I still don't know who that one is."

"Maybe some crimes are just meant to go unsolved. Billingsworth is right about that. It's a secret. It's something that has been a secret for more than a hundred years. I'd say that it's time to let it rest," he suggested, trying to comfort her.

"But I feel like we were so close. Like all the answers were right there. Answers which I'll never be able to find again."

Charlie sighed. "I don't know much about Jack the Ripper, but what I do know is that these things have a way of coming around. Who knows which secrets would destroy people and which wouldn't. I think he's doing right by sealing the room. Now no one will be able to turn this crazy thing into a crusade."

"I've been pursuing it for so long. I don't know what to do now."

"That's easy," Charlie answered, taking her hand. "You are a teacher, and I am your student. Don't let yourself lose track of what you set out to do. And as I remember it, we have a play to write."

"Scene one," said Arden touching Charlie's face, pulling him towards her into a kiss.

When they finally separated, she said, "I think we should go home. And write."

"Yes, write. We have a lot of writing to do," replied Charlie, kissing Arden again.

"Yup. The play won't write itself, you know."

They left the pub and headed back towards Arden's apartment.

## Chapter 51

**"We are such stuff As dreams are made on, and our little life Is rounded with a sleep."**

**- *The Tempest***

Peter woke up with a start. That cute nurse was in his room again, fluffing his pillows. He smiled at her.

"Thanks, luv," he said.

"Is there anything else I can get for you, sir?"

"I'm no sir. Me name's Peter, and yours?"

"Catherine. Kate for short."

"Nice to meet you, Kate," he said, taking her hand.

She blushed for a moment, and then she went back to straightening his sheets. "You've been out for a while," she said, smiling. "I hope you've had some good dreams."

Peter thought for a moment. The realization caused a strange sense of peace.

"Not a one," he murmured. "Not a single one."

THE END

# About the author

Originally from Los Angeles, CA, Naomi has been living and working in London since 1999. She has been writing forever and concentrated on theatre in most of her education receiving a BA in Art History and Theatre from Franklin & Marshall in the US, an MFA in Staging Shakespeare from Exeter and a Post Graduate Degree in EU and UK Copyright Law from Kings College in the UK. She is also the author of *By Page* about her year as a Congressional house page in Washington DC and the play *Madman William* which has received critical acclaim in both the US and UK. She is the co-author of *The Plain and Simple Guide to Music Publishing (UK Edition).*